The Free Traders

The Free Traders

by F. F. Nicholls

CHARLES SCRIBNER'S SONS   NEW YORK

The Free Traders

1. THERE was a lantern hanging from a beam in the middle of the barn, but it did not light up the interior, for the barn was too vast. But the light struck, flickering, on the shoulders, hats and arms of the thirty or so men who stood beneath it; here a shiny bald head shone for a moment, there an eye glittered sharply in the pale wedge of a face.

The men had been waiting a long time, and they were tense; they stood about in knots, talking little, talking in a low grumbling monotone. Occasionally there was a burst of high, false, nervous laughter. Nearly all wore the grubby knee-length smocks of the English country laborer of the 1790's, but one small group kept apart, cut off from the others by their fantastic appearance. These six men were clad head to foot in black, and they had even sooted their faces, making the whites of their eyes gleam by contrast. All the other men carried long stout walking-staffs; these six carried sticks which were weapons—heavy polished murderous "swinglers" or "bats" of holly-wood; and propped against the trusses of hay on which they lounged were long shotguns. These men alone waited silently, calmly, indifferently, with the air of men about their normal business.

Then, over the hum of voices, came the sound of a quick

step outside; the wooden latch clicked, the door hinges creaked, and two men entered. All the heads turned, and silence fell. One man stepped forward from a group and touched his hat brim respectfully to his employer, Mr. Robert Gibbons, of Peasmarsh Farm, Rye, in Sussex. Gibbons, tall, prosperously dressed, looked around masterfully, counting silently. "Thirty-three? One short, George."

"Yes, sir. Job Setterfield. Took sick, sudden-like. His old boy just come over."

There was a jeering laugh from the men around, and Gibbons snorted, "Took sick! Took coward, more like. Well"—he raised his voice slightly to command attention —"so much the worse for him, stupid clown. Now then, lads, are we all ready? A few hours' hard work, a little hazard perhaps—not much—and there's half a guinea in your pockets. A week's wage, eh, for two hours? And a good dollop of tea that'll bring you in another crown!"

There was a stirring of feet and an exchange of wide grins and chuckles before the tall farmer held up his hand again. "A moment, lads! Listen now to your orders for tonight: now, Jacob Higgins is due in half an hour in the *Two Brothers*. We meet him on the beach opposite the farm; the cargo is brandy in half-ankers and dry goods—tea." He turned to a lanky, white-faced youth in the nearest group, and poked him playfully in the chest with his riding-crop. "Here's young Noakes, George. Don't know what a half-anker is, I'll be bound. Well, it's a five-gallon tub, my boy, of the best French brandy. They'll be roped in pairs. Heavy, but get them up over your shoulder, you'll carry them twenty miles, eh, lads? If you had to?" There was a respectful laugh, and the farmer paced easily, casually, among them. "Now then, when you go out of here it's over the road, down the beach— not a sound or a glim of a light, mind you—get your tubs, then make haste along the road toward Camber. You'll go

8

across the marsh to the Kent Ditch, and along the bank to Guldeford Corner; there you'll find the wagons waiting, and that's all that need concern you. Then back for another load. Once we've got it all loaded George will give you all your half-guineas and your dollops of tea. Farewell now, and good luck! Stay! One more thing: if the gaugers or the dragoons should arrive, I'll blow three long blasts on this whistle. Scatter if you hear that, and make your own way across the marsh to the wagons. I'll be with you, and I'm bringing my pops"—he pointed, unsmiling, at the flintlock pistols gleaming in his belt—"I keep these for the damned interfering gaugers, but if any man runs without my signal, or drops his tubs to run faster—by God, I'll pepper him too. Don't, for your own sakes, think that I won't. I've done it before, lads, I've done it before." He pulled out a gold watch, and his face relaxed again. "Very well, then. Time to go, lads."

As the smocked figures jostled in silence by the door, Gibbons went over to the strange group of black-faced men who lounged in the straw. These men were different from the eagerly respectful laborers; they did not rise at his approach, and the man whom he addressed continued to chew a straw, his face set in an habitual and unpleasant half-smile. "Well then, Catt," said Gibbons, "all your batmen ready and willing?"

"Ready this hour."

The farmer swallowed, ignoring the insolence of his tone. "You'll need to divide your men, half on the Camber side, half on the New Romney road. There are dragoons at New Romney, and as you know, our friend Tucker the gauger lives there, so you yourself must be in charge that side."

Catt made no acknowledgment of the order, but rose to his feet, followed by his men. "A guinea each, and a dollop of tea?" he said.

9

The farmer clamped his jaws so that the muscles bulged. "When the wagons are loaded. And one thing must be clear, my friend. There's to be no bloodshed if you can help it."

Catt grinned at his followers, and spat as he turned away: "If we can help it."

Gibbons flared up at last; he seized the batman's arm and swung him round. "No bloodshed, Catt! I'm a free trader, not a butcher. I know how you do things at Hawkhurst, but you are working for me now. If three of you can't overpower and tie up one old riding-officer, say the word and I'll get others. Anyone else you can scare off—with a crack on the head if you like. If the soldiers come, fire two shots in the air, and clear out. But if Tucker should bring a few Customs House men with him—why then, maybe, an ounce of lead's the only way. God knows the damned gaugers are fair game. D'you mark me, now?"

Again Catt made no reply other than a shrug. He shook himself free and stalked off in the wake of his men, muttering to them: "Damn his eyes, I say. Plug the lot, and have done with it—that's our way."

They went out. Gibbons found himself trembling with suppressed anger. "Tom!" he called sharply, and from the shadows came his son, almost an eighteen-year-old copy of himself, with the same high color, good looks, tall build and insolent assurance. "Tom, I don't like the look of things. This fellow Catt would slit his grandmother's gullet for sixpence. You'll be up on the sea wall to give the signal; keep an eye on that gallows-bird for me. Rot him, I've a mind to plug him myself and save His Majesty the price of a rope!"

They made their way to the door and walked through the yard and down the farm lane toward the road and the sea, Gibbons resting an easy, fatherly hand on his son's shoulder. "Well, my lad, you've lived easy for eighteen years on the profits of the trade. You're sitting about in school, learning Latin like a gentleman when most lads are following a plough and keeping a family. It's time you learned the business yourself. By the way—your sister's indoors, I take it?"

"No, Father, she went out half an hour ago or more——"

"The devil she did, the little vixen! Small wonder you two are twins—damned if I know which is the more stubborn and disobedient. I told miss to stay indoors. The less the women see of the business the better. Then they can't chatter."

"But she's only gone to Camber, to take some liniment to old Mother Fagg. She's got rheumatics."

"What if she has? That whining old crow could wait till morning. Confound the minx! I'll shut her up on bread and water for a week. We'll see how Milady likes that!"

Ten minutes later that part of the shore of Romney Marsh where Kent and Sussex meet was as still as death. Tom Gibbons, standing on the sea wall, could see nothing of the thirty tub-carriers who sat along the base of the wall a few yards away, nor of the batmen, who would now be in position in the roadside ditches. Looking inland, he could just make out the flat leveled line where marsh met sky, and looking out to sea he could follow the sweep of the shore of Rye Bay. It was a perfect night for a "run"—moonless, cloudy, yet fine; not much surf on the shingle, for the westerly was gentle and off-shore.

Inside, the boy was one knot of tension. His mouth was dry, and he found himself swallowing and licking his lips often. The night wasn't cold, yet he kept shivering. Smuggling had gone on around him ever since he could remember, but until now he had been kept in with the women while goods were being run. Now at last he had an im-

11

portant part to play—and it was nearly time. He took out his tinderbox and extracted the flint and steel. "Look for the blue light in the southeast, and then give them a 'flink' with your flint and steel." And there it was! A brief, dim blue light, much nearer than he'd expected. Clink! went the steel against the chunk of flint, which he held up high, so that a shower of sparks fell past his face, blinding him for the moment. "Abel!" he called softly, "pass the word —she's in sight. Half a mile out."

"Right, Mas'r Tom."

Five minutes later Tom and his father heard a muffled order, saw the big lugger suddenly open up broadside-on, and heard the rattle of her cable in the hawse as she let go. Then from across the water, over the gentle suck and hiss of the waves in the pebbles, they heard voices, heavy rumbling bumps, and a loud splash, followed by a succession of smaller splashes; then the vigorous rhythmic creak and splash of oars. A smaller black shape detached itself from the hull of the lugger. Robert Gibbons grunted his satisfaction: "Ah, here she comes—the skiff with the sinking-rope. Not a man to waste time, Jacob isn't."

"May I come down now, Father? I can carry two tubs with the best of them! Please, I beg you!"

"Not this time, son. I need you here. Humphreys saw a revenue cutter in the offing today—the *Fox*, he thought it was, beating down-Channel. She might run back in the dark, and you're our best pair of eyes." With a reassuring thump on the shoulder, his father slipped nimbly down, landing with a clatter on the shingle. He called to Humphreys, and all the tub-carriers scrambled down as the skiff crunched into the pebbles at the water's brink. The hard, urgent labor of the run began: the bow oar in the boat flung a small line to the men ashore, who began hauling in feverishly. After a few moments a stouter rope appeared and the men lay back, dug in their heels and took the strain of a long haul. Still there came from the lugger the sound of continual splashes.

All at once there was a quiet rustle of foam and a faint breathless cheer from the laborers. They had seen the first pair of tubs bobbing and gliding through the surf—the first of a great line of tubs and oilskin parcels that stretched snaking from the *Two Brothers* to the shore. As soon as the first tubs grounded Gibbons slashed the seizing that held the pair of tubs to the rope, and carefully pocketed the cut spun-yarn. It wouldn't do to leave the beach littered with evidence of a run. Then he helped Abel Marling to shoulder his load and the laborer went stumbling off up the shingle.

"Come, then, lads," he said. "Who's to be next? Keep together. Don't trouble your heads about the damned gaugers —the batmen are there to deal with them!"

Standing up there, alone on the sea wall, out of all the work (the man's work) and excitement, Tom felt hurt and sullen. His first run, and still he was treated like a boy. True enough, it *was* time he lent a hand; he'd dreamed of it for years, dozing over Latin in school. But not as a poor puppy at apron strings, as a *man!* Hang it, he could carry tubs further than that starveling Noakes, any day. Look for the *Fox!* Father was no better sometimes than an old woman. Ten to one the *Fox* was swinging around her hook in Chichester Harbor by now.

Soft! What was that! Hoofbeats approaching along the New Romney road! He could hear a murmur among the batmen, could hear them shifting position. Some action at last! If he kept down on the seaward side of the wall he could work back to the east beyond the batmen's position, and see who it was.

He crept along the rough turf bank, past where the batmen waited in silence, back toward the lonely sound of the hoofbeats. When he was perhaps twenty yards beyond the watchers he climbed to the top of the sea wall and lay flat.

The horseman, whoever he was, was in no hurry, but approached at a steady walk. Not many used this quiet road across the marsh, even in daylight; after dark, there was only one possibility, surely—the gauger, Riding-officer Tucker, covering his regulation four miles of coast. The boy grinned in anticipation in the dark; if it was Tucker, the batmen had no cause for alarm; the poor old gauger was a standing joke in Camber for his caution. The ambling horse kicked a spark from the grit and Tom could at last make out the bulky figure of the rider. Yes, it was Tucker! And he was nervous too, for his head kept switching about. Then he reined up his horse with a scuffle; Tom glanced to the left at once and saw why. Three tall black figures were drawn up across the road, their holly-wood swinglers at the ready.

The batmen laughed jeeringly as the riding-officer halted, and Tom raised himself on his elbows, grinning broadly. The center of the three batmen stepped forward, and Tom heard Catt's voice, thin, cracked and ugly: "What cheer, my old gauger! Where you off to, then?"

"I am riding on His Majesty's business, my man, and I order you to clear the highway." The words were firm, but the voice was sadly wavering and uncertain.

The only answer was a shout of laughter; and Catt gave the man on his right a great shove on the shoulder. "You heard what the officer said! Clear the highway, you wicked wretch!"

Tucker touched his horse with his heels, and made an indecisive move forward as the batmen, who had clearly been drinking while they were waiting, reeled about laughing. Catt at once seized his bridle and spoke with a horrible kind of jesting venom: "Now then, Henry, we got business

14

here, and we don't want no interference. You just turn about face and get home to yer little bed; else you got a choice of a cracked skull, a trip to France, or a belly-full of lead. Which is it to be, fat-guts? Eh?"

Up there on the wall, Tom joined in the cruel laugh as the elderly customs man wheeled his horse and galloped off, but he felt, somewhere within him, a twinge of shame and pity at the old man's humiliation. After all, what *could* he do?

And then he became aware of a sound that they had all somehow overlooked until now—the sound of another horse, approaching at a spanking trot along the flinty New Romney road.

2. So smartly was the newcomer approaching that he was almost opposite Tom's post before he met Tucker, and Tom could hear every word they exchanged. The batmen formed up again in a silent row as the two horsemen halted together. The newcomer had stopped at Tucker's entreaty, but he and his horse seemed impatient; Tom could hear the slap of his whip against his boot, and the scuffling hoofs of his fidgeting horse.

"You must, sir, you *must!* I beg you!" Tucker's voice sounded almost tearful. His manner seemed respectful, and Tom soon saw why. As the newcomer's horse pranced around Tom could see his rider full front; there were the white facings and glinting buttons of a dragoon officer! Dragoons! The one enemy that even the most lawless smuggler had to respect! Father must be warned! Why hadn't Catt fired the warning shots? If only his father had let him have a pistol!

He was about to leap to his feet to dash down to the beach when his own folly struck him. The officer was alone; perhaps he wasn't even on duty. A good thing Catt had kept a cool head, then! He strained his ears to catch the dialogue again. The stranger was speaking, his voice clear, high, aristocratic, arrogant: "For the love of God, my friend, stop

16

gibbering and whining. Why must I not go on my way?"

"There's a run, lieutenant——"

"I see. And what may that be?"

"A run. The free traders——"

"Smugglers, my man. Let us call things by their right names."

"Aye, sir. Smugglers . . . Well, they're running goods ashore across the road——"

"Very well, then, sir. You are of the Customs Service. Stop them and arrest them. Or if you cannot, go home and leave troubling me."

Tucker mustered up what dignity he could. "I am returning to Romney, sir, to report. I can do no more. But you must not——"

The lieutenant cut in icily: "You may be the terror of the smugglers, my friend, but you have no power to forbid an officer of the Crown to go about his business on the King's highway. Now, if you please——"

"But, lieutenant, you are new, are you not, to this area?"

"I am. My family's estates are in Oxfordshire. What of that?"

"It means, sir, that you do not understand these men. They are lawless—and they carry fire-arms. The three men who stopped me will doubtless be waiting——"

"Do you suppose, my friend, that a man who has charged uphill against a line of French muskets is going to be put off by a parcel of Sussex boors? Besides," he added with a vain, unpleasant little laugh, "a dragoon officer does not keep a lady waiting, even a farmer's wench. Good night, my prudent friend."

With this he wrenched his mount sharply around, dug in his spurs and galloped off towards the three silent figures that stood between him and Camber. Tom thought for a moment that he would use his speed and the weight of his

17

charger to bear them down, but evidently he thought there was no need for such methods. At any rate, by the time Tom had run back along the wall the officer had stopped, and was once again arguing, this time much more angrily. He heard Catt's voice first:

"You'll have to go back, sir."

"I will do nothing of the kind, fellow."

"For yer own good I'm telling you, Captain, same as I told the old gauger. We got private business here."

"I'm a dragoon officer, my man. I'll trouble you to take your dirty hand off my bridle."

"Well, sir, like I was saying, it's for——"

"So! Very well, then. *There's* for you!" The rider raised his heavy crop high and slashed back-handed clean across Catt's face. The batman flung his hands over his face and went down and back with a yell of agony. There was a storm of cries and blows as the lieutenant struck savagely at the faces and hands of the other two men. And then, from the roadside, high and clear, the terrible sound of Catt's voice, shaking with fury: "*Stand away, boys, stand away!*" Then the roaring blast of a shotgun, and the officer, struck in the chest at point-blank range, was flung like a rag doll sideways in the road. The charger reared high on his hind legs and cantered nervously up the road, but he was trained to the flash and bang of muskets, and soon he swung off the flints on to the grass, and put down his head to graze.

Dead silence fell upon the little group standing about the fallen man; every man still frozen in his place, Catt still pointing the gun at the space, now empty, where the rider had been. They were hard enough men, but even they— even Catt himself—were shocked by the suddenness, the brutal finality, of what had happened.

Tom forgot all his orders and, dashing up, thrust himself, morbidly curious, right into the ring. So horrible was the sight, however, that, by the time his father came running up, he was sitting, sick and shivering, on the roadside grass. Robert Gibbons did not spare him a glance. "Catch that horse and bring him back here," he said. Then he reached out his huge hand and caught the front of Catt's coat. "It was you, wasn't it, Toby Catt? Eh? Be damned for a filthy, murdering cur!" He thrust the batman away in loathing, so hard that he crashed to the road, and as he lay there Gibbons pulled a coin from his pocket and pitched it full in his face. "There's the last guinea you'll ever get of me, Toby Catt. Now get your lousy hide out of my sight."

Catt rose, and drew his hand across the dark angry weal that slanted from temple to mouth. "Look at that then! Pretty, ain't it? Might have lost an eye! You can storm and shout, farmer, but what was we to do, eh? The whelp wouldn't stop."

"Wouldn't stop!" the farmer snorted contemptuously. "Three great ugly lubbers and they couldn't make him stop. Couldn't pull him down and cool him off with a tap of a swingler!"

Catt thrust his face forward furiously. "All very well to talk. Your hide's safe, thanks to us. What about his sword and his pistols? I don't care to be chopped up for dead mutton, not me."

"Look at him, then, Catt! No, don't turn away—look at him—what's left of the poor devil. Where's his sword?"

"Pistols, then. In his holsters," said Catt sullenly.

Without a word Gibbons went to the horse, now nuzzling into Tom's hand for scraps of grass, and up-ended both saddle-holsters. They were empty. His voice was like a stone when he spoke. "Nothing. He was unarmed—off duty. Just a young man off to meet a girl or drink a glass. And brave bloody murderer Toby Catt has to blow him to pieces." He made a violent flinging gesture with his arm. "Now clear out of my sight, back to your hole in Hawkhurst! And if I clap eyes on you again it'll be the assizes for you, and I'll come with the rest to watch you dancing six foot up. And by God I'll enjoy it!"

A few moments later Catt and his two fellows were receding silently along the Camber road, and the foreman George Humphreys and Skipper Jacob Higgins advanced out of the shadows to take their places around the slim crumpled figure. The skipper shook his head gravely. "A bad business for you, farmer; a bad business. This is a swinging job, if it's found out. They won't stomach lieutenants getting plugged, not they. A gauger or two perhaps—they don't signify; but a lieutenant of dragoons—and a high-flying young dandy by the look of his lace—that's another matter. A bad business, right enough."

Tom looked at his father and saw, to his great relief, that he had not only got himself under control again, but had the look of a man who could see a way out. He roused himself from a long reverie, and turned to Higgins. "No use croaking like an old raven, Jacob. To my thinking, there's only one answer. The man must—*disappear*."

"And, you see," went on Higgins gloomily, "a young fellow like that will likely have gentry for relations. They'll turn this parish upside-down, they will, and it's a jig in the air for Master Catt when they find this."

"Aye, aye," said the farmer impatiently, "but mark me now, skipper. As I was saying, this young blade must vanish from the face of the earth. Nothing found, no evidence; no evidence, no trial, no noose. With your help it can be done."

"My help, farmer? Hold hard a minute! I don't choose to wear a hemp cravat, I thank you. No more do my lads. I'm keeping out of this affair. Besides, we shall be heaving up in ten minutes."

Gibbons shook his head with a grim smile. "Too late for

that, Jacob. We're all parties to it now. These old men in wigs would as lief see a row of us dangling as one. The noose is around all our necks if this is found out—yours, mine, even that boy's there!"

Tom felt his stomach give a lurch of fear, and he found his hand caressing his neck. "Around all our necks!" It had been bad enough feeling utterly sick, miserable and ashamed at a brutal killing done by one of his father's men; now he realized that this deadly cold fear which gripped him would be part of life from now on—something which might be forgotten for a while, but which would come surging back at the sight of a dragoon, or a gun, or even at the soft warm muzzling of a horse's nose in his palm.

And there was another thing—a phrase which the dragoon had used, which he had been trying to forget, dismiss, thrust out of his mind: "even a farmer's wench"—a farmer's wench who would be "waiting". Mary? A rich and arrogant dandy like this man might call her that. But where could they have met? Wait, there was that ball at the Assembly Rooms in Rye last week. She had seemed secretly excited after that, he remembered. And this errand of mercy to Mother Fagg . . . Twins are different from other people. They can never quite keep a secret from each other; he had felt at the time that this was a rather sudden awakening of charity towards someone known as the most cross-grained curst old shrew in twenty miles. There, then, was the worst misery of all: Mary was the "wench" who was waiting, who would wait in vain now. The death of the dragoon would have to be kept utterly secret, twin or no twin.

"Tom!" His father's voice made him jump. "I'll take that horse. Run back to the farm; bring a lantern and a spade. Off with you!" He arrived back five minutes later breathless and bewildered. A spade?

"Good. Now, see here." His father led him to the spot

21

where the lieutenant had died. Several of the laborers had arrived and the body now lay, muffled in sacks, by the roadside. In the middle of the road there was now only a large dark stain on the whitish flint. "Now then, set to work! Dig up every single stone with the slightest mark of blood on it, and put it in this bucket. Amos is fetching a bucketful of clean flints from the yard. Lay those in place of the others and stamp them well home. And make haste; old Tucker may have given the alarm, for all we know."

"Not he, farmer," said Higgins. "Poor old chap's hearing's gone, and he'd have been a mile off when Catt fired, if I know him."

"Aye, but we can't be sure. Now, the tubs are all ashore and the skiff ready? Come then, boy. Tck! Tck!" he clucked to the horse and led him away. "It's a midnight swim for you, poor beast, and then an ounce of lead in your skull."

"Dear Lord," grumbled Humphreys, "it's a crying shame, sir. I'd get fifty guineas for that mount in Ashford Market."

"Aye," said Gibbons over his shoulder. "And sixpenn'orth of hemp to go with it."

The magnificent horse breasted the sea wall and picked his way skillfully down to the beach. He laid his ears back at the treacherous sliding of the shingle beneath his polished shoes, but obedience had been drilled into him and he followed Gibbons quietly into the sea. The skiff, which was now afloat, with Jacob Higgins in the sternsheets, backed gently towards the man and the horse, a heaving-line was made fast to his bridle, and as the sailors gave way easily with their oars, the horse plunged himself forward and began to swim in the boat's wake towards the silent lugger. Soon after, there came the sound of a muffled shot, and soon after that, the sounds of departure came drifting across the water—the steady clink-clink of chain, the thud of boots on deck, the squeal of blocks.

22

"Well, so much for that." Gibbons swung round. "Humphreys!"

"Sir?"

"I told those dolts to muster here after the wagons were loaded. Are they back yet?"

"Aye, sir. All waiting."

Gibbons crossed over to them.

"Now then, men, you all know, I daresay, being a parcel of tittle-tattling old women, what's happened tonight. You know I wish no harm to any man, barring Toby Catt. It was an accident. But to the judge"—he lowered his voice and leaned forward, pointing in turn at the scared, gaping faces—"to the judge, I say, you, and you, and you, and you are all guilty of his murder. Every mother's son. *Guilty!*"

He paused to let his words sink in. "But never fear, lads, we'll give them the slip yet, and die old men in our beds, eh?" There was a feeble chuckle among the frightened men. "Remember, when men ask you questions: you were in your beds; you saw nothing, you heard nothing. No matter who asks you—your own wives even—mum's the word. And if any man"—his eyes traveled around slowly to look into each white face—"if any man should be tempted to think of earning a few crowns by blabbing, he'll remember, I hope, the way of us free traders with spies and informers. Think on that, my lads, think on that."

3. Tom's breath was labored, his back breaking with the strain, his arms filled with a dull agony of fatigue. He was digging, digging; he had been digging for a long time, so that now a great black hole gaped in front of him. He was about to plunge his spade yet again, when he suddenly stopped in horror. There was Mary, looking at him, calling to him, from the bottom of the hole. He might have killed her with the spade! Why had she put that ragged, filthy red tunic on over her dress? He turned around to explain why he must stop digging, but the huge black cat which had forced him to dig in the first place was angry, and bared its teeth. In despair he turned to his work again. But now his sister had gone from the hole, and in her place was an old judge, his face set under the wig in lines of iron severity. He must know about the whole business, for he was calling Tom by name, calling time after time: "Gibbons. Gibbons! GIBBONS!"

Then a hand plucked at his shoulder; the judge and the hole disappeared, and he was struggling into consciousness, and looking point-blank into the face of Iorwerth Lewis, M.A., Master of Rye Grammar School. The master was furious; his sharp, fierce young Celtic face was flushed, and his

24

dark eyes seemed to bulge out from their sockets, as they always did when he was in a rage.

There was a raucous laugh from his score or so of classmates as Tom sat up, rubbing his eyes and feeling foolish.

"Well, sir?" said the Welshman, and waited for an answer.

The heavy, stunning drowsiness ebbed away from Tom's brain and eyelids, and he faced the master sullenly. "Went to sleep," he said, adding reluctantly, "sir."

"Indeed? Indeed? And why, pray?"

"Up last night." He grinned slyly, sidelong, at his neighbors. "We had a cow sick." There was a roar from his cronies. They knew well enough why Tom had missed his sleep, half of them had fathers, uncles or brothers who were also heavy-eyed today, and nearly all of them had come from homes well stocked with run goods. Booth, the buffoon of the class, had to try to cap Tom's witticism: "'Twas a valuable cow, sir—a Schiedam. She gives down five gallon a time."

The laugh stung the master to fury, and he slammed his hand down hard on Tom's desk, his face white and moist. "Silence! I will not be answered in this way! I was led to think when I came to this place that I should be teaching the classics to the sons of gentlemen; instead, I find myself wrangling with ill-bred louts!"

The boys fell silent, stirring angrily in their places, exchanging dark looks. How different it had been with old Mr. Lamb! The old man would loll in his chair or pace the room, teaching if he felt like it, telling long improbable stories of his army life if he did not. This Welshman, on the other hand—he seemed to look for trouble, to run his head straight at it. His appetite for work was ceaseless, fierce, yet he had thrown away all Mr. Lamb's canes, relying on his fiery personality, his bitter tongue.

"Yes. Louts, I say!" He glared right into Tom's eyes.

"Gibbons, I demand an apology from you for your gross ill-manners. Well, sir?"

There was a long horrible silence. Tom felt his black misery, turned into rage and resentment against the Welshman, choking him. His clenched hands trembled, longing to take the man by the throat and hurt him savagely. At last his chair scraped back and he stood up heavily, grudgingly. "I apologize, sir," he said sullenly.

"Very well," said Lewis, adding bitterly, "The charm of your manner has quite won me over. And now, if you please, we will proceed with our Virgil and the misfortunes of Laocoon. Gibbons, you will construe, if you please. In case you are in doubt, the line is number thirty-four: '*Hic aliud maius miseris multoque tremendum. . . .*'" And again, he could not resist a gibe at his enemy: "You have the correct book, I take it?"

Tom flushed again with helpless rage. Only a little runt, this Welshman. He could knock him down with one blow. "I have." He took his eyes off the master and studied the tattered, inky text.

He looked dully along the line—"*Hic aliud maius miseris multoque tremendum obicitur magis atque improvida pectora turbat . . .*" Something was wrong today; usually (though he would never have admitted it to his friends) he liked the pretty, ingenious way the Latin words fitted together, glove-tight, clicking into place like halves of a well-made joint. Today those same words seemed endless ranks of meaningless symbols; this work should have been prepared last night, but the excitement of the run had driven Virgil clean from his head. Still, the habit of obedience was strong, and he began stumbling through:

" 'Hic'—er—'This'——"

"No!" said Lewis abruptly.

" 'Here'——"

26

"Wrong again. You have prepared this passage, of course?"

"Yes."

"Very well, then. Good. We await your English version, sir. I will begin it for you: 'Hic'—'At this time . . .' Proceed."

"'At this time another'. . . er . . ." His mind was working at last, ahead of his hesitant words, and when he at last understood the lines the cruel irony of their meaning struck him like a hammer—like a stern, blinding light: "At this time there occurred to us miserable men another thing, and one much more to be feared, which distressed our unthinking minds——"

He got no further than that, for the words were like a judgment from above; it couldn't be just a coincidence— it was an exact description of what had happened to them all. The awful horrors of the night reeled round in his head— the sharp dead crack of the dragoon's whip on Catt's flesh and bone, the blast of the gun, the bloody rags twisted in the dust. His head throbbed; he felt sick and hot, then clammy and cold in rapid succession. He reached out for the desk as he swayed. His face was pale and glistening.

Lewis looked suddenly concerned. "What is the matter? Are you ill, my boy?"

Tom gritted his teeth; he didn't want anyone to be kind to him now, especially not this damned Welshman. "No, sir," he said.

"Then why the halt? The line is not unduly difficult, surely?"

"I cannot do it, sir."

"One of the best Latin scholars in the school? *Cannot* do it?"

"No."

Lewis bit his lip, summoning his patience. "We will construe it word by word, then. Now: '*maius*'?"

Tom stood, his eyes on the book, his face impassive, no longer even appearing to think. There would be a head-on clash with the master, he knew; but somehow that was what he wanted—anger, blows, disgrace; they suited his present mood better than love or pity. Toby Catt was to blame, of course. Well, he was out of reach; but Lewis and his father —them he could plague and torment; they were to some extent in his power. Let them hurt him as much as they could; it might help to ease this horrible feeling of guilt. Mary had looked pale and set that morning. Nobody else had noticed, but he could see that she had cried herself to sleep. Where had she waited for the dragoon? Had she heard the shot? Was that why she had given him that long searching look as he rose from his half-eaten meal?

All these thoughts coursed through his head as he stared sullenly at the book. Lewis sat at his high desk, looking at him. Utter silence—unnatural and tense—had fallen. The younger boys, set to work on their own, had stopped their shuffling, murmuring, nudging, and stared at the master, gauging the new man, seeing how he would act, what he was made of. The silence was unbearable.

Suddenly Lewis's patience snapped. His taut face had become flushed; with a gesture of passionate anger he brought his fist down on the desk-lid with a crash that made the ink-well jump and the chalk-dust rise; that made the watching boys catch a breath in delicious fear. "Lout! You dare to defy me! 'Maius!' A word you learned a full five years ago. This is casting pearls before swine indeed! I order you to construe the word—at once!"

The watching boys exchanged glances, but Tom merely raised his eyes to stare straight at the master in open defiance.

Lewis looked at him and at the other boys and felt disgusted—with Gibbons, with the rest, and with himself.

What kind of education was this? Dumb insolence on one hand, yells of rage on the other. He rose abruptly, and at the scrape of his chair he could sense the small sigh of expectation. He walked up to Gibbons and stood over him; then suddenly he turned his back and paced away: "Very well, then, Gibbons: Tomorrow morning at nine you will bring a fair copy of a translation of the first two hundred lines of the Aeneid, Book Two. If this is not perfect in every way, Gibbons"—he swung around again to look at the boy—"I shall be seeing your father about your future in this school."

No one spoke, but after the dead silence there was a movement of relaxation, anticlimax, even disappointment. This was not old Lamb's way; there was clearly not going to be a flogging. But they all understood the veiled threat of expulsion, and they looked at Tom to see how he had taken it.

He felt tormented, frustrated; the Welshman had outwitted him. He was to be left with his bitter resentment after all; Lewis would go on with the lesson now and ignore him for the rest of the day. But there was something in Lewis's nature that made him run himself into trouble; he had won this skirmish, yet he couldn't leave it at that: to crush his opponent still further he made a remark which he at once regretted: "In any case, Gibbons, I am dubious about allowing felons to remain in my school."

Tom leaped to his feet and leaned forward furiously. "Felon? Do you call me a felon, sir?"

"I most certainly do."

The master was back, sitting perched behind his high desk. Tom walked out to face him across it. That dead silence had fallen again. "And what crime do you reckon I've committed?"

"Smuggling. I may be a newcomer to the coast, but I know well enough what this Schiedam that your fellow-lout mentioned is: Dutch gin, highly prized by local sots, and imported illegally by smugglers."

"What proof have you got that I'm a free trader?"

"None. It is merely my considered opinion. And I did not say 'free trader,' I said 'smuggler,' just as I would say 'highwayman' and not 'gentleman of the road.' "

There was an angry murmur among the boys, for almost all their families profited from the runs, as helpers or buyers of cheap tea, tobacco or spirits. Booth's father, for instance, was a grocer, whose cellars were crammed, the year round, with French brandy, Dutch gin, smuggled tea and tobacco. Booth, too, jumped up. "You didn't ought to call free traders criminals! My father says 'tis the Government are the criminals, putting taxes on goods so that poor folk can't afford them!"

Lewis was carried away now by his passion for argument, and seemed to have forgotten that he was schoolmaster to these boys, and that both Booth's and Gibbons's fathers were governors of the school. He jumped up, his eyes blazing furiously. "And I tell you that your smuggler friends are traitors as well as felons!" There was a concerted yell of angry abuse from the boys, but he was too angry still to see how far things had gone wrong, and simply shouted them down: "Where do the French get gold from to pay for their wars? Who carries their secret letters to their agents in England?"

The yelling rose sharply to a new peak, then suddenly stilled, for the boys saw that Tom had reached out a hand to seize the lapel of the master's coat. Tom liked the feel of the cloth in his grip, liked the thought that in two minutes he could beat this man into insensibility. He glared, his lower lip stuck out, down into Lewis's eyes, expecting the sudden blanch, the quick swallow, the incoherent stutter of fear—the signs he had seen so many times when he had swaggered among the smaller boys. Instead, the master, now fully in control of himself, looked down at Tom's hand, then straight into his eyes; there was a faint twitch of a smile on his lips, and not the slightest trace of fear in his eyes.

"Very well, Gibbons. Very well. That settles it, then. You will remove your hand from my coat, and then yourself from this school. You are suspended until I have seen your father, and have received the fullest of apologies from you. Now go at once."

Tom was taken aback and flustered. He lowered his hand, but stood his ground, sneering, "Oh, and who's to make me go if I don't choose to?"

Lewis snapped his fingers at a small boy sitting near the door. "Hurrell, ask the porter to step this way, if you please." He turned to Tom again: "You will see, I think, Gibbons, that you will only make a greater fool of yourself by showing further resistance."

Tom looked searchingly at him, then turned to scan the faces of his classmates, but they were too awestruck to offer him any encouragement. With a snort of disgust he strode through the door, head held high, and slammed the door behind him with a thunderous crash.

"Line thirty-four," said Lewis calmly, picking up his book; "'Hic aliud maius miseris multoque tremendum . . .' Dunn, construe, if you please."

4. MR. MOLE, Solicitor of Rye, was a fine handsome man, with his powdered hair drawn back fashionably to form a pigtail; he looked a proud, strong, dangerous man, too, when he leaned forward in court to bully or trap some bewildered poacher. But now, facing the furious Gibbons, he showed his real nature—his eyes watery from spirits, his chin weak, his smile ingratiating.

"This fellow Lewis—that damned Welshman at the school—he will have to be dismissed!"

"The master dismissed? You are not jesting, Mr. Gibbons?"

"I am *not*, sir. The fellow has shown himself utterly unfit for his post. You will summon a special meeting of the governors for tomorrow, and we'll send him packing."

"But, Mr. Gibbons, what has he *done*? We cannot simply dismiss him unless . . ."

"What has he done, sir? Well, yesterday my jackass of a son fell asleep during school—he had been busy the night before, you understand."

"I do," said the lawyer with a smile, "but most profitably employed. We had some of the new Suchong tea at breakfast today. Delicious!"

32

"Aye, well, he set him an imposition for that—two hundred lines of some Latin rigmarole. Very well, I don't complain of that. The lad shall do it or I'll flay the hide off his back. Lewis may have renounced the birch, but I haven't. But then the puppy goes on to call his pupils—your boy too, I suppose—louts and swine, my son a felon; and the folk of this town canting humbugs. To round it off he says that all free traders are traitors and winds up by expelling my son. My son!"

"Bless my soul! Your son? Expelled? That does seem hasty, to be sure——"

"Aye, well two can play at being hasty." Gibbons suddenly thwacked the desk with his crop, making the ink-stand —and the lawyer—jump violently. "Come then, Mole! Send out to the governors! Eleven o'clock tomorrow at the school will be suitable to me."

"But I need the chairman's authority to——"

"Lord Tillingham's in London, as well you know. Booth's vice-chairman—he'll authorize it. Can't rest till I see that damned upstart Welsh prig on the road."

Mole's cautious lawyer's mind had been turning the problem over. "Of course, you do realize, don't you, Mr. Gibbons, that, legally speaking, expelling a boy is quite within his rights? As governors you have no power to interfere in the daily discipline of the school. The deed of trust makes it quite plain that——"

"To hell with the deed of trust—and you too, Mole, if all you can do is croak. When you could scarcely feed your family I got you this job as Clerk to the Governors; I made you Clerk to the Justices, Clerk to the Workhouse Board, Clerk to the Harbor Commissioners. Dammit, I expect some service from you for that!"

Mole was crushed, mumbled apologies, thought for a while, then raised his forefinger in triumph. "I think I have it, sir! Would you not say that Mr. Lewis is a proud man?"

"Aye."

"And stubborn?"

"Aye, for aught I know. Get to the point, Mole."

"Yes, sir. Now, we cannot *discharge* him without putting ourselves in the wrong. But . . . you gentlemen can pass a motion of censure on him, demand apologies, undertakings for the future, and so on. Do you not think, sir, that if the motion were sufficiently strong, and . . . ah . . . humiliating, that he . . . ?"

"That's it! Capital! That stiff-necked beggar wouldn't stand for it! He'd resign and save us the trouble!"

Mole spread his hands complacently, smiling. He produced snuff, and then a bottle of Madeira. When the farmer went out ten minutes later he paused in the doorway, grinning. "I'll go around and muster the lads for tomorrow. I'll make sure the half-wits know what to think and say. Do you draw up the motion of censure. And make it hot, Mole, make it red-hot!"

"I will, sir, I will. He deserves it. He's no better than this dragoon fellow!" He smiled across at the farmer, and was puzzled to see his face strangely still, purple with a dark flush.

"Dragoon? What dragoon?"

"Oh, some young puppy of a lieutenant, sir. Deserted last night, they say. There's a wench in it somewhere, depend upon it. Related to Lord Tillingham, I hear. Watch out for him sir, sir—there's a price on his head!"

Two days later, Gibbons was standing in his dry, neat yard, enjoying the summer morning sun and an after-breakfast pipe of run tobacco. He was planning the day's work with George Humphreys; the pipe-smoke hung still and bluish above their heads as they talked. They broke off and turned towards the gate, smiling, as Tom appeared pounding up the track; the boy threw his satchel over the gate and followed it with a springy vault.

"Ah," said George. "I was like that, one time o'day. Never opened a gate I could jump over."

"No school, Tom?" said the farmer innocently.

"No! And no Mr. Lewis either. There was only the usher there. We've all got to study at home until they get a new master. Lewis has gone!"

"I know," Gibbons chuckled complacently. " 'Twas I who put the powder behind him. Rot him for a canting Methodist scoundrel!"

The boy swung around, open-mouthed, astonished. "But hold hard! You made me sweat over his damned two hundred lines of Virgil last night till my very brain ached! Till past midnight! And all the time you knew he wouldn't——"

The two men roared at him until he had to give in and laugh too. "Discipline, you puppy, discipline! Eh, George?"

"Right you are, sir!" said George. "Discipline, Mas'r Tom. And I suppose if this old Latin tackle does you young scholards so much good, you'd best give thanks for a double helping!"

On either side of him the ruddy handsome Gibbons faces grinned. He wasn't to know that behind each laugh there was a hard knot of uneasiness. Tom was remembering his last view of Lewis when he came into the classroom to collect his books from his desk—the livid face, dark haggard eyes, the firm impassive voice with no hint in it of weakness.

Robert Gibbons knew he'd triumphed and was trying to enjoy it, but somewhere inside him there was a nagging unease. Somehow at that governors' meeting the winners had lost, the loser won. How the man's eyes had blazed! There had been little flecks of foam on his lips as he spoke his last words to them: "Very well, gentlemen. I think I see your purpose at last. Leaving out all the canting hypocrisy, Mr. Gibbons has decided to take his revenge upon me for disciplining his son, and all of you follow him like sheep. Three months ago I was delighted beyond measure to be appointed to carry on the work at this fine and ancient foundation; now, after today's pitiful display, gibbets and racks would not persuade me to stay a day in a school run by such a parcel of ignorant, craven, greedy carrion as I see before me." Then the slamming of the door—and silence among twelve glum and confused men.

Humphreys broke in: "By the way, sir, I seen all the chaps last night. They'll all be down the barn ten o'clock tonight. I got ten more, as you said there'd be extra goods. Where's the run to be, sir?" Usually no two runs were in the same place.

"Where should it be but opposite the farm?"

"But look 'ere, master——"

"What's the fear now? Old Tucker? That decrepit old woman?"

"There's the dragoons——"

"They'll be busy elsewhere, from what I hear. And besides, hasn't the sergeant at Romney had a tub of Geneva for himself and his lads every run this half-year? Why should he trouble us?"

"Ah, but there's been packs of 'em about the parish— strangers—officers—from Hythe—asking all manner of questions."

"George, you're getting timid as an old maid. The dragoons are hereabouts because they think a certain person has deserted. Come now, don't start whining, man; you're the only one I can trust until this young sir comes of age. Then we'll see what he's made of."

They both looked at Tom—the master tall, in fine linen

shirt and tight breeches, coatless on that warm morning, switching his boots with his riding-crop; the foreman short, wiry, tough and lined, his short carroty hair dusted with grey at the temples, his crooked hard brown hands folded on his long carter's whip, for as well as being foreman he drove a team of four fat gleaming Shires. He grinned at Tom, then at the farmer: "Father's footsteps, I s'pose. He'll be the—fourth, is it?—Gibbons to dodge the gaugers, I'll lay."

"Aye, George. Sixty-five years now, we've been in the game. It was 1729, my grandfather told me once, when the first gin came to Peasmarsh. But be that as it may, we must settle tonight, and then today's work. There's a yard-full of hands standing idle, and nine o'clock struck already! Is the grass in Twelve-acre ready for the scythe yet?"

"'Tis greenish yet, and short in the straw. Couple o' days of sunshine . . ."

"Aye, aye. Finish off the turnips, then, while 'tis dry. We'll have a load of faggots from Iden Wood for the stack-bottoms. But don't go over there yourself, George, or there will be precious little hoeing done here. I've to be out on business. Take your team to plough the fallow ground in Ditch Meadow. Then you'll be able to squint over the hedge now and then."

Humphreys turned away, knuckling his forehead, and Gibbons put a heavy arm across his son's shoulders and smiled, lifting away the days of sullen depression and resentment that had divided them. "You'll come with me, Tom?"

The boy smiled with relief to feel the barrier going down between himself and the father he admired so much. But the smile faded; something still worried him. "Father, there's something Mr. Lewis said . . ."

"Huh! That canting Welsh rascal!"

"But he was not a fool, Father. . . . And there was something he said . . ."

"Well, out with it!"

"About smugglers being traitors . . . giving the French gold . . . and carrying messages for their spies in England . . . ?"

"Ah, that old yarn!" Gibbons snorted. "Traitors, indeed! I wonder if Mr. damned Lewis knows there are King's ships manned alow and aloft by smugglers—and there are no smarter tars in the Navy."

"Aye, but the gold?"

"Well, Tom, goods have to be paid for, and the only thing the Frenchies will take is gold. Can't be helped. As for the spy messages, as I said, that's just a dirty old lie, spread by such as hate us. Men like Jacob Higgins are as loyal to King George as any man. They wouldn't help Boney's spies. There's always been free traders on this coast, and always will be; all the while the Government robs poor men by putting taxes on the good things of life. It's true there are a few cut-throats and murderers like Catt and the Hawkhurst gang, but most of us—well, we're just family men plying a trade."

Tom smiled back at his father as, stooping, they made their way through the low back door. The chat with his father had made him feel better, but there was still a little knot of unease within him; he felt in his arms still the jarring scrape of a shovel on a dry road, and as they went into the kitchen his sister sprang up from the chair where she was shelling peas and swept past them, her face white and set, her eyes haggard and withdrawn. How much *did* she know or guess?

The night was fine, starry, but dark, for the moon was only the finest of curved chips of light in the western sky. On either side of the Romney road the land lay flat for miles; to the west the marsh with the light smudge of a feeding sheep here and there, and the random gleam of water from a ditch; to the east the featureless desolate shingle desert and the far-off muffled roar of the sea. Riding-officer Tucker felt the cool stillness, felt that the sound of his ambling horse's feet must be heard for twenty miles, along with the ceaseless, tuneless, formless whistle that his fear produced.

The old man paced along, muttering and whining his thoughts between the stretches of dreary whistling. Like any lonely, old, ill-paid, unsupported riding-officer of the day he had cause enough to complain. But underneath, under a layer of shame and guilt, was the real reason for his misery. Like the Peasmarsh gang, he was walking round with a blood-secret; apart from them, only *he* knew (or was pretty sure of) the truth of the lieutenant's death; like them, he was silent because he dared not speak; but with him the haunting figure of terror was not a judge but the dark, harsh form of Toby Catt. True, they might string Catt up. Might! But if they didn't . . .

Forget it, Henry mate. Here's a quiet night, anyway. Nearly at Peasmarsh Farm and not a soul about; well, like enough they'd hold up for a fortnight . . . after that. And a good job.

The old man jogged along. The sea wall was at his left elbow now—too high to allow him to see over it the wink of a blue light, the double shadow of the lugger's canvas. And the marsh road ahead was far too black for him to see the row of blackened faces watching him as he approached.

George Humphreys gestured towards the rider, his eyes gleaming white as he grinned, put his finger to his lips for silence, and lifted his holly-stick. The customs man came quietly, serenely, on until he was almost up to where they stood in the ditch; then he stopped, suddenly sharply attentive. His practiced ears had caught, faintly over the low roar of the surf, the rattle of an anchor-cable and the squealing of halyard blocks as the lugger's yards came down with a run.

And while the poor old man sat irresolute, his horse reined in, both ditches exploded in savage din of whoops, shouts, dancing. Back-handed, and with all his strength, Humphreys brought the cruel knotted leather thong of his carter's whip down to land with a sharp whistling snap across the horse's rump. The terrified gelding, young and strong, reared high in the air, screamed high and shrill, and tore off into the darkness towards Camber, his rider clinging to his neck. Henry Tucker had lost his left stirrup and slumped further and further to the left as the horse dashed from sight.

George Humphreys dabbed his streaming eyes, held his aching sides, stifled his laughter, and said, "Pore ole 'Enry. Won't 'ardly stop before 'Astings!"

Tom came down, yawning and scratching, late to his breakfast next day. Well, he had earned a late lie abed, with those five hours of back-breaking work in the cold dark, hustling along the marsh paths with a hundredweight of gin slopping and sloshing in the barrels across his back. And all quiet except for poor old Henry Tucker—what a caper he'd cut, pelting past them at full gallop, yelling like a fiend, hanging on to his horse's neck, his wig and hat shaking off to show his shiny, bony old skull. They had all laughed themselves weak at it, until Father, getting over it first, had had to be pretty sharp with them all. Well, it was as comical a sight as a man could hope to see.

He was brought up at the door of the kitchen by his sister, who was coming out with an armful of starched linen. He smiled at her shyly, embarrassed, for since the dragoon affair they had been like strangers. "Ah, Puss," he said, using her childhood nickname, "so you're stirring early——"

"The bold cavalier," she said, cutting him short, her face white, tense and bitter, "one of those brave night-prowlers!"

"What's this? What do you——"

"How many bold cavaliers does it take—thirty or forty, with your sticks and guns and swinglers—to kill an old man?"

"Kill? You mean——" He was genuinely astonished and alarmed.

"Riding-officer Tucker. Aye, kill, as near as makes no difference. To lie all night in a ditch with a broken thigh, to be found at dawn drenched in the dew—it's not a light matter for an old man. But what of that?" She spat the words at him coldly. "The gin and tobacco are safe."

5. It had been dark under the elms of the long straight driveway, and Iorwerth Lewis had to screw up his eyes as he came out into the open sunshine on the lawns fronting Tillingham Place. The warm, faintly golden stone of the Jacobean façade struck the heat back at him as he mounted the imposing front steps. He did not need to ring, for a hulking footman in powdered wig and livery of crimson and white was lounging in the porch, staring down insolently at this dark, fox-faced caller in the plain brown coat, who could not even afford a horse, it seemed.

However, Lewis was in no way put out, and spoke crisply and confidently: "I wish to see Lord Tillingham, please."

"By appointment?"

"No. I should like you to tell His Lordship I am here. My name is Lewis. I am—or was—the master of Rye Grammar School. My business with your master is exceedingly urgent and important and——"

He broke off as the butler, starchy and self-important in black, appeared through the open door of the hallway. "What is this person's business, John?"

"Wishes to see His Lordship, Mr. Capper."

"Appointment?"

"No, Mr. Capper."

The muscles of Lewis's jaw clamped, and he tapped his hat impatiently against his leg. "Have the goodness to convey my message to Lord Tillingham. My business is, as I said, most urgent."

The butler, plump, soft, beautifully shaved, ran his eyes contemptuously up and down the schoolmaster's neat threadbare clothes. "Ah, sir, many of our callers say the same. His Lordship is at work on state papers, and left orders not to be disturbed. If you would care to leave a card—if you have one . . ." He rolled his eyes slyly towards the footman, who grinned.

Lewis flushed darkly with rage, and the South Walian in him came out. "Look, man, I am staying by here until you've taken my message to His Lordship!"

The butler gave that sly complacent smile again, shook his head gently, and then nodded towards Lewis. "Remove this person, John."

The footman, grinning delightedly, carefully shot his cuffs back. Lewis looked surprised, then, as he understood, faintly alarmed. Well, that wasn't surprising, they thought; but what he said was puzzling: "No, man, don't do that, now! There's all these steps here!"

The butler held out a spotlessly gloved hand to the footman. "A moment, John. You are leaving, then, my friend?"

This time the Welshman looked puzzled. "I? No indeed. Not until I have seen him."

"I see. To work, then, John."

The bear-like footman lunged out his great meat-like hands to grasp the small man's coat. Dammit, a little whippet like that could be carried out bodily. But somehow he never touched that coat, for just as he was about to do so, Lewis swayed back, yielding pliantly like a willow switch, and John found himself wrong-footed, off balance, teetering forward. And then fingers like steel wire caught hold of his right arm and, as the intruder spun to his left, wrenching at the arm, John found himself, yelling, in mid-air. He landed with a dead, rib-cracking thump on the third step, and rolled the rest of the flight down to the gravel.

As he struggled to rise he found Lewis standing over him, a concerned look on his face. "You are not hurt, now, are you? Told you, I did, not to do it. I was afraid this might happen. Lucky I didn't put my weight into the throw, or you'd have gone all the way in one go. Arm all right?" So concerned was he with his fallen opponent, that he did not notice the butler yelling hysterically, or the two gardeners rushing up, brandishing forks. They had nearly reached him when, from a window above, a commanding voice cut through the babel.

"Capper!" At once there was an awed silence, all the servants freezing in their tracks. "Capper, what is the reason for this din and brawling on my doorstep?"

"Your Lordship! Your pardon, m'lord. This person here was attempting to force his way in. When John tried to evict him he was——"

"I am aware of what happened. And who are you, sir, to assault my servants at my own door? What business have you with me?"

"My name is Iorwerth Lewis, my lord. I am, or was, master of Rye Grammar School. I wish most urgently to inform you of the circumstances of my dismissal."

"And does that justify an attack on my servants? I am liker to send you to the magistrate than speak to you myself."

"As Your Lordship pleases. But I attacked no one, and I received nothing from your servants but the most intolerable and boorish insolence." There was a gasp and a wide-eyed wondering look between the servants at this, for they

44

had never heard the master replied to in such a way, not even by gentry, let alone a schoolmaster. They waited for the sky to fall.

Instead, however, Lord Tillingham said curtly, "Capper, show Mr. Lewis to the library."

The library was a sunny room, the sunbeams outlined faintly by dancing specks of dust, the warmth drawing out of the packed shelves the smell—so delicious to Iorwerth Lewis—of old books: a mixture of dust, musty paper, aging leather. His Lordship still stood, a silhouette against the leaded panes, but he swung round as Lewis entered, and came to meet him, acknowledging his awkward bow. Now that he was close, he did not seem so formidable—just a handsome, drawn man in his fifties, his white hair combed back to form a pigtail, his clothes quiet but beautifully cut.

"So, Mr. Lewis. Pray be seated." There was the slightest twitch of a smile on his lips. "If your Greek prose is of the same quality as your Greek wrestling you are indeed a nonpareil among schoolmasters. While I cannot approve of your actions, at least I will apologize for my butler's impudence; he is an old woman and a pompous prig into the bargain."

"I must apologize too, my lord, for such an unseemly disturbance . . . but I do not care to be so easily fobbed off."

"Quite so. And where, pray, did you learn to defend yourself—if 'defend' be the word!—so effectively?"

"In Merthyr Tydfil, sir—my home. My father is a clerk in the office of the iron works. When I was ten I won a scholarship awarded by the ironmaster, Lord Dowlais, to a school in Brecon. Most of my time I was the smallest boy in the school, and on the holidays in Merthyr I was the only lad of my age in our street who did not work in the furnaces. Perhaps your Lordship will understand how I was treated?"

"Indeed. After all, I was at Eaton myself."

"I owe my skill to a Cornish boy. Believe me, it has been

45

dearly bought. But my youth had been made so miserable by fear of bullies that on my fourteenth birthday I swore an oath to myself never to give in to a swaggerer, but to learn to fight him at his own game." He smiled. "It has cost me so far two broken arms, three collar-bones and a rib."

Lord Tillingham looked straight at him over the leather-topped desk, unusually impressed by the pale firmness of the face, the burning fires in the large dark eyes. "So, to business, Mr. Lewis?" He listened attentively, toying with a quill, while Lewis told the story of the Virgil lesson and of his interview with the governors, and, when he had done, thought for a few moments. "H'm. A sorry enough business, I agree. Yet, to be strictly accurate, you were not actually *dismissed*, Mr. Lewis."

"As good as."

"Yes. As good as. The intention was clear enough. Gibbons is a fine man in many ways, but crude and impetuous. But again, I consider that you yourself were at fault in airing your political opinions in a lesson on the *Aeneid*, and in so roundly abusing your pupils and their fathers."

"I know, my lord," said Lewis, flushing. "I offered twice to withdraw the remarks, but they would have had me lick their boots."

"Exactly. Which you, very rightly, refused to do. But if all is settled, why call on me?"

"You are the Chairman of the Governors, my lord. I wished to give you my account before you heard lawyer Mole's version. And I thought that you might be moved to intervene on my behalf. In your position . . ."

Lewis stared hopefully straight into the great man's eyes, and was amazed to see him lower his gaze, flush and fidget uncomfortably in his chair. He helped himself to snuff before replying: "Yes. Well, Mr. Lewis, I have no doubt that that is what should be done, and normally I should be most eager to act. However, there is, as you know, the Parliamentary election to consider."

"Parliamentary election? What in the world has that to do with this affair, my lord?"

"You have been frank with me, Mr. Lewis, and I will be similarly candid. The fact is that I have my two members ready to serve my purposes in the Commons—good purposes, Mr. Lewis—and generally the voters of Rye accept my nominations without question. This year, however, the seats are being contested by two Whig interlopers. There are about fifty voters in all, Mr. Lewis, and a good dozen of them are governors. . . . You see my dilemma?"

"I do indeed," said Lewis contemptuously.

"And do not be so quick to curl your lip, my friend! I wonder whether, in my place, you would be anxious to throw away a place in the government, and the fruits of years of effort, just to save a foolish young hothead who cannot control his tongue?"

Lewis stood up, his face taut with anger. "Quite so, my lord; who would? Well, I have always read that politics is an unsavory business. Now I see the proof."

Lord Tillingham jumped up too, white and shaking in fury, but just as he was about to speak there was a knock, and Capper the butler entered, bringing a letter on a silver salver. The nobleman took it, motioning Capper to go and Lewis to wait. He read it, pursing his lips gravely at its news; when he looked up, it was clear that his quick anger had gone. "Bad news, Mr. Lewis. Your smuggling friends again; Riding-officer Tucker was set upon last night and is not likely to live long. To leave an old man gravely injured in a ditch all night! Faugh! I have more reason to hate these fellows than you suppose, Mr. Lewis. They are no friends of mine. There was my nephew's disappearance a week ago —well, we shall never know the truth of that, but I'll wager he fell in with the batmen, as they call them. 'Tis a cursed trade."

"And yet like enough the snuff in your fingers now came here in their luggers."

Lord Tillingham nodded and sighed. "As you say, sir, Capper buys it for me; I do not ask where."

"Do you see now, my lord, why I spoke as I did to those boys? This 'free trade'—it is an evil cancer, penetrating and rotting away every part of the community. It drives otherwise decent men like Gibbons into brutal lawlessness and anarchy, and brings the whole machinery of the law into contempt and ridicule."

"That is certainly true. I am one of His Majesty's Commissioners for Customs, and recently we have seen our officers convicted for defending themselves, while murdering rascals are let off scot-free and grinning. No Sussex jury will ever convict a smuggler, for fear they find their houses burned about their ears." He sighed again. "It is enough to make one despair."

Lewis had been standing gazing thoughtfully out of the window while the earl spoke. Now he seemed to come to a decision and swung round. "My lord, it seems I cannot be a schoolmaster here. I owe you an apology for my hasty and thoughtless remark. Let me make amends by offering myself as riding-officer in place of Tucker."

The great man's eyebrows rose in astonishment, and he shook his head vigorously. "You? Riding-officer?"

"I could do the job, my lord."

"I have no doubt of that, Mr. Lewis. But since I have failed you once today I shall not do you such a disservice as to place a young man of learning and taste in such a hard, ill-paid and dangerous post as that of a riding-officer. Long night vigils, Mr. Lewis, in all weathers, and the only certainty at last is an ounce of lead in your brains. Now, I have a far better idea: I can offer you at least three months' work as my librarian. You see these shelves? Crammed with books and documents, many valuable, some priceless, some utterly worthless. There is all of Livy, Tacitus, Herodotus, Horace, Pliny, Lucretius, and so on. There is a Caxton Chaucer, and bundles of Anglo-Saxon writings from the Abbey." He gestured out of the window to where among the splendid oaks of the park, a herd of long-horned Sussex cattle fed quietly, the sun glinting red-brown on their well-fed hides. "Together with my pedigree Sussex herd, my books are my pride and joy. But what time have I to sort and catalogue them? I need a scholar, Mr. Lewis, to do it for me, and I believe you are that man."

"I will do it, sir, gladly. But only if I may take the other post as well. I can do both."

"You can, sir. But what in the devil's name prompts you to such a course? I cannot see one reason for your offer."

"I could give you many, my lord: there will still be Virgil to construe and boys to rule when I am fifty; and you may think I have a score to settle with the men who have served me this trick. But my real reason is neither of these—it is simply a certainty that this is the task destined for me at this moment. To try to help to cure the county of a disease that is rotting its heart away."

"It is not a post for such as you, I repeat, sir. I cannot consider it."

"You have a replacement for Tucker? A good man?"

Lord Tillingham stroked his chin, deep in thought, and pondered frowning for some time. At last he shook his head with a rueful smile. "I have never met a young man, Mr. Lewis, who was better at getting his own way. So be it, then: I will see that you are offered the post of riding-officer. You will not, I think, wish to have it long."

He held out his hand with a smile, and the two men, so

utterly apart in their rank and breeding, exchanged a look of mutual warmth and respect. Outside the door, Capper straightened from his position at the keyhole, shook his head, and crept off with a face of astonishment.

6. "Don't forget, then, George, to send Abel Marling and his boy in for the sheep about three o'clock. I shan't buy more than four dozen. Let him go! Hey, Prince, hey!" The foreman let go the bridle, the big dun gelding threw himself into the traces, and the light gig went curving out of the gate, spurting gravel from under its high varnished wheels.

Gibbons snatched a glance at his son and grinned. "A fine day, Tom, for a drive to market!"

"Aye."

"They tell me that that Welsh sniveler went whining to Lord Tillingham yesterday. Much good that will do him, hey? His lordship is a good Sussex man!"

"Aye."

"And they do say that he's to be riding-officer after Tucker, but I don't believe a word of it. Just a fairytale from that old keyhole-listener Capper."

"Aye. But——"

"But *what*? What the devil's the matter with you?"

"Nothing, Father," said Tom, staring blankly ahead.

"What in God's name is the matter with my family? There's your sister—a cursed sullen witch, forever turning her back on me with scarce a civil word, and your mother forever huddling and whispering in corners with her. Now you, lolling about idle, and dumb as a damned monk! Now, out with it! 'But' *what?*"

"Very well then, sir. Lord Tillingham may be a Sussex man, but he was also uncle of the dragoon."

"Dragoon!" Gibbons cursed and gave the horse a cut that made him toss his head, scattering flakes of greenish froth. "If I hear about that damned fool again! So he's still sticking in your gullet, eh?"

"He and Henry Tucker. They say he's in a high fever."

The farmer lashed out vindictively again, the cord snapping on the shiny flank. "That craven old gauger! Don't lay *that* at my door, either! 'Twas not I who whipped his horse! And how would we know he would take a fall? Dammit— you laughed yourself with the best of them!"

"I know, Father. I remember that well. That is why I feel——"

"Ashamed? Of me?"

"No, not of you. Of the whole crew of us. Of the whole sorry business. Why cannot we be just farmers? 'Tis a good enough trade, surely?"

"Farmers! Faugh! What do you know of it? All the wealth and comforts you've seen have come from the free trade. And I've determined that you shall have a gentleman's up-bringing, as good as Lord Tillingham himself had."

"But I don't *want* to be a great man like that. I'm——"

"Pah! The devil! What do you know about life? You'll do as I say. And you'll be grateful to me later—I promise you that."

Tom sat silent, his mind confused and bewildered. Father was so certain, so assured. If only you could be like that at eighteen! Wasn't he usually right, too? After all, he was a good and kind husband and father—stern but kind. He was no Toby Catt. If he said the trade was the right thing for them . . .

The gig spun along in the dusty sunshine, passing laden wagons, barking sheep-dogs, and their panting, frightened flocks, all making for Rye market. The boy's gloom lifted in the warmth and noise; he glanced sideways, caught his father's eye and flushed awkwardly. "I ask your pardon, Father. I've been a sullen lout. But I'll do as you say, day or night."

Gibbons roared, his quick anger gone, and fetched the boy a tremendous thump with his free hand. "That's more like my old Tom! Now look here, boy, I can see what the trouble has been: things have been dull here—and not pleasant—eh?—at times? It does you credit, Tom, to have a heart, but when a man is in a business, why, he must sometimes do harsh things—not meaning any harm to any man, but just as a soldier must level his musket at the enemy front rank. He's got no grudge against any one Frenchman there, but his captain says 'Fire!' and bang!—he fires! And then there are accidents, too. Time you had a change of air. I've a scheme for you that will give you a fine sea trip, teach you the business, and help me into the bargain. . . ."

That night Mr. and Mrs. Gibbons sat before the last of a wood fire. The farmer warmed his nightcap of cider by stirring it with a hot poker; his wife, a quiet, patient, handsome woman, stitched away steadily at a sampler. Now and then her eyes flicked shrewdly across at him; she knew he had something to tell her—something he was not anxious to talk about. Well, sooner or later he would say it. He cleared his throat awkwardly: "I've been thinking, Ethel . . ."

She smiled to herself. At last! "Yes?"

"That boy of ours . . . leaving school seems to have unsettled him. He mopes about like a cluck hen."

"*Something* has upset him, Robert, certainly." She lowered her work and looked at him in a way that made him drop his eyes hastily.

"Eh? What d'ye mean by that, woman?"

"Something that you know about and I do not. You will not tell me what it is, I know, and I shall not ask. Perhaps it is the same thing as upset Mary."

"What? Nonsense, woman, nonsense!"

"Indeed? Both of them were blithe enough until the run a month ago, when you and Tom came back white as sheets, with not a word to throw at a dog."

"Aye, well, all that is done with," he said, abruptly. "In my judgment the lad needs a change, so I'm sending him to Dunkirk as freighter for me."

"To France? When?"

"Saturday night. The *Two Brothers* is due on the beach at eleven. He will go with her when she sails."

"To France? When we are at war with the French?"

Gibbons snorted and laughed. "Tchah! War! What difference does that make to the free trade? The m'sieurs are all the gladder to see us, Ethel. They need English gold to pay for their powder."

"But there are revenue cutters. Tom is a young lad to have cannon balls shot at him."

"Revenue cutters! Cannon balls! Don't forget the lad is sailing with Jacob Higgins, the wiliest skipper in the Channel. And the *Two Brothers* has the heels of any cutter we've seen yet. No, there's no danger, and 'twill do the lad a power of good. Great idle lubber!"

Dark. Utter dark between the thick yew hedges. Dark and dead silence. Only the dry scrunch of gravel under Riding-officer Lewis's feet, as he approached Camber Church along the private pathway from Lord Tillingham's house. The church itself showed as a black mass against the starlight; now he was near enough to pick out the tiny glints of metal on the side door—the shiny handle, studs and hinges reflecting the minute gleam of the stars.

In his pocket he still had the scrap of paper with its illiterate scrawl—*Bee in Camber Church ten Thursday nite. A Frend.* He had found it yesterday morning shoved under the door of his Rye lodgings; the "frend" had come and gone in the night without a sound. As it chanced, that was the last night he had spent in those lodgings, for he now had a room at Tillingham Place. It would be safer for him there, Lord Tillingham said.

Lord Tillingham had also said it would be folly for him to keep the appointment, but Lewis's stubborn streak had come out again. There had been quite a scene. "This note, my lord, may be a trap, but it is much more likely to be from an informer trying me out. God knows I despise such men, but if they are the only way—and I believe they are— then I will deal with them—aye, and pay them well, too."

And here he was (half wishing he had listened to his master), easing open the heavy door, which squealed on its dry hinges and swung open. Not a sound or a glimmer of light inside. The air smelt dead and stagnant, a blend of incense and crypt-like mustiness. He walked slowly to the center aisle, wincing at the loud sound of his steps on the echoing flags. He stood quite still and listened, listened so intently that he could hear the tiny creaks and ticks of the ancient roof-timbers under their load of lead.

Suddenly, with a shrill grate and a deafening bang the side door by which he'd entered was slammed shut. He felt the blood rush to his scalp and tingle there, as his heart almost stopped with the shock. Why in the world had he not taken advice and brought a pistol?

For a few moments there was another eerie silence, then

the sound of a slow step and the harsh croak of a voice. An old man's voice. Malicious and sly. "Mr. Lewis?"

"Aye."

"Speak your name, Mr. Riding-officer Lewis, so I can be sure who 'tis."

"I am Iorwerth Lewis: and who may you be, sir?" Lewis found his confidence beginning to return, but had to steady his voice all the same, for his whole body was ice-cold and shaking.

"Nobody with yer, Mr. Lewis? You swear it?"

"Nobody. Once again—who are you? And what do you want of me?"

The old man did not reply at first, but Lewis could hear feet shuffling nearer, nearer, until a groping hand suddenly slithered against his chest, and a skinny claw settled on his forearm. He became aware of the evil warm smell—ale, to-bacco, bad teeth mingled—as the old man thrust his face close. Lewis just overcame his panicky desire to throw off this tattered dusty old bat of the darkness.

"Seth Hewett, I are. Verger o' this church. You don't know me, but I know you. You and me can help each other, sir. You're His Majesty's riding-officer now, ain't you? Got four mile of coast to patrol every night. Can't be in every place at once, can yer? No. Well then, what you need is a feller to let you know about things—when the lugger's due, where the run's to be, and all such as that."

"True. But how are you to know this in advance?"

"Ooh, I shall know, sir, I shall know. They shove me up in a chimney corner just the same as if I was an old dog!"

"Who, sir, who, in the devil's name?"

"Why, my girl Elsie, of course, and her man Abel Marling. Precious son-in-law he is. Out for every run. Comes back full of gin. Can't git up for work next day." He cackled horribly: "Well, we'll see, we'll see!"

"So through your son-in-law you will always know about runs in advance?"

"Aye, aye. They talk as if I wasn't there. And I'll let you know the night before; ten o'clock in here."

"How shall I know which nights I am to come here?"

"Ah, let's see now. I got it: you know the big black marble tombstone? Right-hand side of the path? You can see that from the back of the big house. If I got a message for you I'll leave something—scythe or a spade, say—leaning against it."

"Very well, I agree to that."

There was a short pause before the old man began again, in a cunning whine: " 'Course, I'm risking me neck, sir, every time I see yer. It'll have to be worth my while, like. Same as when you git your prize-money after a capture . . . I mean, you won't forget old Seth, sir?"

Lewis fought down his overpowering disgust, and spoke curtly. "You shall have ten shillings of every pound I receive, Hewett. But if I find you sending me on wild-goose chases I shall see to it that you rot behind bars for it."

"Ooh, there won't be none o' those, sir. I swear it. Only you got to swear too, sir, that you'll never tell a living soul —not even his high-and-mighty lordship—where you git your news."

"Agreed. Now, my friend, you can begin by telling me when the next run is, and every single detail of Gibbons's methods. Leave nothing out, however trivial."

"There is to be a run tomorrow night, my lord," said Lewis next morning, as he and the nobleman strolled among the smooth box hedges.

"Indeed? I will not inquire how you know. Have you made your plans?"

"I have, sir. But they depend upon you, I fear."

"Upon me?" He stopped in his walk, astonished and angry. "How so, pray?"

"I have a plan, sir, but it depends on the help of a man of absolute discretion and . . ."

"And *what?*"

"And some—er—fortitude. . . ."

"In plain words, this ally of yours is likely to be peppered?"

"It is possible, sir, but not likely."

"I see. That is considerate of you! I may return with a whole skin, then?" He snorted. "I have never in my life, Mr. Lewis, met a man so preposterous and impertinent. Really! Do you seriously suggest that a man of my years and position, with boxes of state papers to attend to, should spend his nights creeping round in wet marsh ditches, with rascals banging buckshot round his ears? I have never heard of such incredible insolence."

Lewis flushed angrily and his eyes flashed. "I beg your lordship's pardon. Your help was asked for this occasion only, and the danger and discomfort would have been slight. But I will make other arrangements. I regret I must take my leave."

He had swung round and strode ten paces away before he was halted in his tracks by a laugh from Lord Tillingham. "Lewis! Hold hard a moment! Hang the man—he boils over like a pan of milk! Did I say I *wouldn't* play soldiers with you? Did I? Damn the state papers—just give your new gauger his orders."

7. IT was a fine calm night on Camber Beach, so calm that the tiny waves only gurgled and sighed on the stones, sucking so gently at them that all the waiting tub-men could hear the splash of the lugger's anchor, the rattle of the cable as she rounded up. Tom and his father stood on the sea wall, where the master-smuggler had been giving his "freighter" (or agent) his instructions. He waited until he heard the rhythmic splash of oars, then whistled quietly to the waiting men, who clambered over the wall with a low cheer and ran down the yielding pebbles. Tom started to go with them, but his father caught his arm quietly. "No, don't go, lad! George can manage. Stay with me tonight. Have you everything straight in your mind, now? Duchamps will send a man to meet you; agree to no more than five shillings a half-anker, with a free tub in every twenty, the tubs to be slung in pairs. The rascal's been asking six shillings lately, and he may try it with you, seeing that you're young. Don't have it, Tom. Tell him there's plenty more liquor merchants in Dunkirk, not to mention those in Fécamp, Calais and Boulogne. Remember, 900 half-ankers of Geneva, 300 of brandy. No tea this trip. Perhaps you'll—— Ssh!"

He broke off, and they stared at each other; the sound of

hoof-beats could be heard along the New Romney road. He whistled low and sharp between his teeth to the batmen in the ditches, and they growled back, "Right!" to show that they had heard too.

"D'ye know, Tom," said Gibbons excitedly, "I've heard this daft story again about your schoolmaster Lewis being the new riding-officer. Can't be true, surely? Well, we'll see in a minute, anyway."

"It will be a chance to pay off old scores," said Tom vindictively. "See if he can gallop faster than old Tucker."

"We'll see what he's made of first, Tom," said his father grimly, his hand on his pistol butt. One of the batmen crept out of the ditch into the road, and his polished swingler gleamed faintly.

The rider was nearly up to them, trotting steadily ahead. Tom felt his breast almost bursting with hatred of the Welshman who had humiliated him in front of his schoolmates. Now he'd pay for it—if it was him! If only he had a pistol—or even a stick. Never mind, there were half a dozen to deal with him. The fool, to thrust his head into a hornet's nest like this! Let him suffer for it, the sneering Methodist prig!

The batman stood up boldly now, causing the horse to halt, throwing his head back sharply. Well, the rider was a gauger, for Tom could make out the tricorn hat, the gleam of brass buttons. There was a heavy silence for a second, both sides motionless. Then at last one of the batmen jeered: "Go on 'ome, gauger, 'ooever you are. Git orf out of it!"

"Clear the road, my friend, in the name of His Majesty King George!" Tom's heart leaped in amazement—it was Lewis! It was true! I wonder, Tom thought, how he'll shape up. He didn't seem like a coward—but then that was against a few schoolboys. What about grown men, clubs and bullets?

The batmen began to close upon him; he reined his horse so that it backed a few paces; then he spoke quietly: "Very well; I have a suspicion that contraband goods are being run here. I shall go, but I shall keep you under observation, and make my report in the morning to the Commissioners." With that, he swung his horse round and cantered away to the east. His words, and his retreat, were followed by a storm of laughter, booing, jeering and whistling. On an impulse, Tom snatched up a sod from the sea wall and flung it, laughing to hear it thud on the rider's back. Some of the batmen threw stones. Robert Gibbons grabbed his son's shoulders and they shouted with laughter, pounding each other's backs and choking.

At last they remembered the night's work, and the farmer gave a long sigh of delight. "Well, George," he said to the foreman, "I can see we'll get on capitally with this fellow. He's taken a leaf out of Henry Tucker's book, eh?"

Humphreys spat contemptuously: "Say what you like, farmer, old Henry was a man when he was that feller's age."

"Ah well, so much the better for us if this one's a creeping cur! Now then, George, the skiff's ashore by now. Get the tubs across to Guldeford Corner where the wagons are. Make haste!"

The batmen were murmuring amongst themselves and chuckling. "Ey! Farmer!" called their leader. "You got good eyes. See that bend in the road? See something black? Look, there's a spark from a hoof! There's our noo gauger, keeping an eye on us."

"Ah!" said Gibbons. "Well out of range, too, or I'd have a mind to pepper the craven rogue!"

Sunday morning was beginning to whiten the wisps of cloud in the east when Tom, a bag of well-pressed clothes on his lap, and a heavy leather purse of gold in his coat, went bobbing across the wavelets in the skiff to the *Two Brothers*. He felt nervous and hollow; he'd been yearning for the excitement of the voyage long enough, but now something had made him feel sick and empty, disappointed. He knew what it was, too: Lewis's pitiful cowardice in front of the batmen and his father. It was very strange: the man was a hated enemy, and yet . . . and yet . . . Tom had counted on him to play the man, at least; to come up to what Tom had expected of him. What an abject idiot he had been! It was a kind of betrayal; instead of a fight with a worthy enemy, they would be just laughing at a miserable clown.

Then the skiff bumped heavily alongside and he had no more time for thought. A man leaned down from the lugger and hauled him roughly over the side on to the deck, where he sprawled like a great fish just landed. The lugger carried a large crew of two dozen hands, and it seemed that in his first ten seconds on board all of them tripped over him. His arm was seized in a strong grip, and he found the lined, harsh face of Jacob Higgins looking at him. "Get below, young Gibbons, you're in the damned way here!"

This was a blow, for Tom fancied himself as a tar. "Nay, I'll help, master," he said. "I'm strong!"

"Aye," said Higgins curtly, "so's a bull calf. Get below, young farmer, before I fetch a rope's end!"

Tom did not venture on deck again until broad daylight, after a brief and unappetizing meal of cold salt pork and biscuit. The berths in the cuddy were now filled with men sleeping off their night of hard work. The fresh warm air smelt delightful, and as he looked around him he thought he had never looked upon a scene so beautiful. They were out to sea. The *Two Brothers* was a long, lean vessel of nearly 100 tons, her ends gracefully raised, her deck flush except for hatches and companionways. Forward, alongside the anchor windlass, was a long black cannon, poking its menacing muzzle through a port; right aft, its twin, the stern-chaser, projected over the wake. She had been built for speed and sea-keeping in all weathers by the far-famed shipwrights of Mevagissey, and carried a vast white lug sail on each of her three masts. The mizzen was stepped so far aft that its sail had to be sheeted to an immense spar, called a bumpkin, projecting over her stern. Forward, she carried three staysails on an equally large bowsprit. On fore and main she carried topsails, and these were both set, for the following breeze was so light that the fiery vessel only crept murmuring through the Channel waters.

They were scarcely abreast of Dungeness Head; the English shore showed as a green, green line ruled to port, though far back across the marsh the morning sun picked out patches of hazy white from the inland cliffs near Lympne. The sea was a vast, smoothly rolling plain of blue, darkened here and there by deeper blue patches where the catspaw ruffled it. Inshore, a cluster of Folkestone smacks rolled lazily at the nets; to seaward, the great ships held majestically on their courses, sailing to London and the Low Country ports from all over the world.

Aft, at the helmsman's side, Jacob Higgins, blowing cheerful puffs from a short clay pipe, was scanning the shoreline with long sweeps of his glass.

Then Tom saw him suddenly check the swing and go back for a second look at a minute white smudge close under the land on the port quarter. To the young landsman it was a mere shapeless blur, but it evidently meant more to Higgins, for he growled out an oath and handed the glass to the helmsman, taking the massive curved tiller while he looked. The man lowered the glass, slid it shut, and nodded grimly to Higgins. "True enough, skipper. *Harpy* it is."

Higgins kicked savagely at a coil of rope and swore: "Must have been lying inshore in the lee of the point. God damn her—she's seen us right enough. You saw, Bill? Just setting her topsail. Run for'ard, young Tom, and tell those greasy idle sojers o' mine to roust themselves out of it!"

The watch below came up growling and rubbing their eyes. They soon gathered, by following the skipper's glass, what was amiss, nor did Higgins leave them long in doubt "Trotter!" he bellowed. "Stern-chaser! Ger her shotted and run out. Lively, you beggarly sots, you! Bosun! Muskets and hangers!"

In a few moments, the deck of the lugger looked like that of a man-of-war. Up came the powder, the muskets and the hangers, or cutlasses. The stern gun was served with naval smartness and skill, for many of the men had been under the colors—many, indeed, were deserters. Tom found a musket thrust into his hand. He took it, for he prided himself on his marksmanship; he got caught up in the excitement. Yet something inside him said that it was one thing to shoot snipe, widgeon or goose, and quite another to put a ball through a fellow Englishman.

He looked again at their pursuer and had a shock; she was much nearer now. He could see now the narrow speck of black hull under the cloud of white sail. Still the *Two Brothers* dawdled maddeningly along, though every sail she had was set. Tom edged towards the stern so that he could hear what the skipper was saying to the bosun, for he felt excited, and yet utterly lost in this strange world, where a tiny smudge miles away put everyone in a frenzy. He knew of the *Harpy*, of course; knew she was one of the smartest and fastest of the Revenue cutters, knew that her young captain had the name of a fire-eater and a terror to free traders, knew that he and Jacob were sworn enemies. The next few hours would be worth seeing!

"Gaining!" he heard Higgins murmur. " 'Od rot 'em, they've just been on the beach for a scrub, and this hooker's as weedy as a half-tide rock." He whistled long and piercingly for a wind. The swells from the southwest, together with a falling glass, told him there was rough weather near; there, down in the wind's eye, was the telltale white bow of cloud. But would it come in time?

Jacob Higgins had lived too harsh a life to feel much in the way of fear; but he had not felt so worried for a very long time. Everything was against him: in a stiff breeze or a gale of wind the lugger's powerful hull would enable her to romp away from the tender, yacht-like Revenue cruiser; or if only they were close-hauled he knew his three great tall lugsails would draw him clear. And here he was, running dead before a light wind that enabled *Harpy* to fly all her kites—square topsail, studding-sails, raffee topsail and such like.

There was a darker line on the sea to windward; it was beginning to pipe up, but of course *Harpy* would get the breeze first, damn her! Through his glass he could now see every detail—the acres of canvas, the small "bone in her teeth," the white foam at her forefoot. As he watched, the cutter yawed up to windward a little to display her flags. There they were—the signal to heave-to.

"Heave-to, Johnny?" he said, for the benefit of his crew. "See you damned first, cully!" Back she came on to her course; he knew what the next thing would be. Sure enough, there was the quick jet of white smoke from her bow-chaser, then a pause while six pounds of shot whistled towards them. The ball fell harmlessly, well short in their wake, and the smugglers cheered derisively, though every man knew it was only a matter of time before she closed the range. They knew, too, that she had a broadside of six guns, and that when she could lay alongside she would make short work of knocking them to pieces.

Still, there was always one hope—the long nine-pounder,

bigger, longer-ranged and much more accurate than *Harpy's* pop-guns. And in Nat Trotter he had a man who had been master-gunner of a seventy-four, a man who could hit targets like a bowler knocking down skittles.

"What d'ye think, Nat?" he asked.

Trotter looked long and carefully at the dainty ship astern, then shook his head. "Scarcely, master."

"There she goes again!" came a cry, and Tom was in time to see shreds of powder-smoke at the cutter's bow. Then the horrible pause while the deadly iron ball hurtled towards them; Tom saw that none of the smugglers took the slightest heed of the danger from it, and he steeled himself to keep standing as coolly as they did. The helmsman did not even look round, but steered as if at a regatta. This time the ball was much closer, no more than fifty yards astern.

"Now, master!" said Trotter. He bent over the gun, a young dark man with the intensity of a scholar in spite of his brick-red tan and unshaven cheeks; the long nine was pushed this way and that with the spike until he nodded; then he trimmed it carefully with wedges and took the lighted slow-match from one of his crew. As the stern rose on a swell he brought the match down swiftly to the touch-hole. The tremendous violence and noise of the cannon's roar was a shock to Tom; deafened, he watched *Harpy* like a hawk. There it was! A small splash just to the right of her!

"Well done, Nat," said Higgins. "You got the range. Come left a shade."

"Aye. The wind's a bit more than I thought," said the gunner. "Look up, here comes another!"

This time there was no cheering, for *Harpy's* shot landed just ahead of them. Higgins chewed his lip, rubbed his bristly chin and looked around. Damn her, she was closing the range fast, and no sign of a breeze yet. Sitting ducks, they were. Muskets and hangers might cheer the hands up, but he

66

knew that *Harpy's* captain knew his business. Why should he grapple them, and risk a hand-to-hand fight with a swarm of fierce and hardy smugglers when he could pound them at his ease for as long as he chose? By disobeying the signal to heave-to they had made themselves King's enemy. He would rake them, dismast them, kill most of them before he boarded. At least, Jacob thought, I would in his place.

The long nine roared again, and he swung his glass on the cutter to watch for the splash. Instead, he saw a sudden flurry of smoke and fragments on her foc's'le, and saw one of her staysails begin flapping to and fro like a banner. He let out a cracked hoot of delight and thumped his gunner on the back. "Gawd bless yer, Nat! You've landed one right smack on his bow-chaser, and parted his forestay too! 'F he ain't careful, he'll carry away every stick and spar aboard her."

The lugger's hands whooped and danced bearishly in delight. The cutter would have to stop to repair her stay, and the bow-chaser would not fire again. The cheering stopped abruptly as they heard in the wind the concerted bang of six cannon. Far from stopping, *Harpy's* captain had risked a complete dismasting by luffing round to starboard until his whole port broadside would bear. Then he bore away again after them, and the smugglers waited apprehensively for the iron shower, their laughter wiped clean off their faces. The seconds dragged, until Tom felt that the shots must have been blanks; then a terrifying low whistle in the air and pandemonium broke loose: there was a whirlpool of splashes, a hole appeared in the foresail, a horrible jar shook the lugger as a ball crashed into her hull, and, worst, of all, in the same instant there was a splintering crash and a high yell of agony on deck. A ball had landed by the foremast, ripping a tremendous groove in the deck before smashing its way out through the bulwark; a giant splinter of teak, flying like a

67

spear, had transfixed one of the foremast hands clean through the body, and he now lay threshing his life away in the scuppers.

That settled it for Jacob Higgins; he could not afford many more broadsides like that, and if he held on his course downwind for Dunkirk the *Harpy* could rake him at her pleasure. If one mast went they were finished. "Down helm, Bill; bring her round to southeast. Aft with yer sheets, yer misbegotten gallows-birds! Two of yer—overboard with that body!" (It didn't do men any good to look at sights like that.)

By swinging around ninety degrees to starboard he brought the *Harpy* on to his other quarter, and the wind abeam. This was what the *Two Brothers* had been longing for; the breeze, freshening well now, began to pipe in the stays, she put her shoulder down to it, and a soft, foamy roar began under her forefoot. The hands busied themselves with the sheets, and two went below to plug the shot-hole. The next broadside from *Harpy* fell raggedly short, only one shot passing through the sails. Trotter banged away with his long nine as fast as he could, and hit her twice in the hull. Two more broadsides were tried, but both fell short, and the cutter ceased firing.

Gradually Jacob brought his powerful craft nearer and nearer to the wind, and gradually the sky darkened and the breeze hardened, until one by one *Harpy* took in all her fancy sails, and even her topsail. With a lashed-up forestay her captain dared not drive her to windward, and she dropped further and further astern. Soon after noon she had dropped so far astern that she disappeared in a rain-squall and the *Two Brothers* was safe again.

Safe, yes, but forty miles from where she should have been, and young Matthew Prigg sent to feed the fishes. Another widow and two fatherless shavers. Jacob Higgins gripped the hilt of the cutlass he was still carrying, and ground out his thoughts to the man at the tiller: "Fine day's work this has been! We'll never get back to Camber on time. By God, Bill, I'll be revenged on that puppy Finch in the *Harpy* one day. I lay I'll make him pay dear for young Prigg."

8. "Starboard! Luff her!" The *Two Brothers* came into the wind and kept her way on for a while, gliding up with canvas drumming and snapping, sheet blocks rattling and dancing in the stiff south-westerly. "Let go!" The anchor-cable roared out, then stopped, finally easing out again a fathom or so at a time as the lugger settled down to her anchor.

As soon as the skiff was launched, Jacob Higgins, Tom, and one of the hands tumbled in (Tom a bit more seaman-like now), and Higgins himself took an oar, making it bend as they rowed the boat ashore. Tom tended the long towline, watching it snake coil by coil over the transom as they pulled away from the lugger.

He could see dark figures on the shingle above the gleaming line of froth where the seas broke. A breaking sea hurled the boat the last few yards, and the men on the beach snatched it up clear of the water as its occupants scrambled out into the surf. Tom had been looking forward to seeing his father again, remembering the way they'd laughed together last Saturday, and the rough warm embrace when they'd said good-bye. He felt he'd done well, that his father would be proud of him. Not a penny more than five shillings a tub, his father had said, and five shillings was what he'd paid, after a great deal of voluble protest in mangled English from Duchamps. And Father would be proud, too, that he'd worked like a slave all the previous night, giving a hand with stowing the tubs so as to make up time. He ran eagerly up to the tall figure standing a little apart: "Father! I'm back again! I got the tubs for——"

His father did not look at him, but thrust him aside with a push at his chest as he strode to meet Higgins; the farmer, savage and morose, seemed not to know he was there. "Well, Jacob, what the devil are you playing at? Be damned for a stupid idle bungler! Two o'clock Tuesday night we said, and here you are at ten o'clock Wednesday! By God, Jacob, I'll find a better shipper, so I will. I'll not pay thirty men to stand about idle all night!"

If he expected apologies from Higgins he was to be disappointed. To have such bitter words after an exhausting day of effort lit the smouldering anger in the skipper. He spat contemptuously on the stones. "So be it, then! Find another shipper and a plague on you! I'll not be spoken to like this by any dung-shoveling cow-keeper. While you people here have been eating good shore vittles and sleeping soft all night in your sheets me and my lads have been cannonaded—and one of us killed. Had to lose a day and a half to get rid of a Revenue cutter, stay up all one night loading cargo, and we've flogged ourselves and the hooker all day to get here. So if it's to be the last cargo, get your flea-bitten clowns to work, and I'll be gone. By God, farmer, you have the soft end of this trade, you do."

It suddenly came to Tom that Higgins's anger was more against *Harpy* than his father, and that in the same way something had gone wrong ashore since they'd left.

"Soft end! Much you know about it, Jacob Higgins. Where think you your last cargo is, pray? In Booth's cellar, perhaps?

Not it! Every last damned drop is in the Customs House at Hythe! Every damned tub that I gave my good gold for! A few runs like that and I'll be a pauper!"

Tom and Jacob were astonished; the quarrel was forgotten. "What! What happened, farmer?"

"That damned Welshman Lewis!" said Gibbons venomously. "Rot him for a dirty cunning meddler!" Tom had not seen his father so bitterly angry since the affair of Catt and the dragoon. "You remember, Tom, just before you left, we were looking at him watching us from the bend in the road? Remember how we laughed at him?"

"I remember, Father."

"Aye, well, the vile rascal had the last laugh on us. It wasn't him down the road there—I don't know who 'twas, for it wasn't one of the other gaugers, either."

"Where was Lewis, then?"

"Aye, where indeed! The dirty meddling cur! Why, as soon as he rode away from us he must have ridden like a madman by some roundabout way across the marsh to Guldeford Corner. He had four Customs House men from Hythe with him by then. What did they do but lie low behind the hedge and watch the wagons loading—watched George and me paying the tubmen—watched us all go. Only the carters were left, and you know, Jacob, how much fight there is in *them*. Jumped out, pistols cocked—'Surrender in the King's name!' Pah!"

"And the wagoners knuckled down, eh?"

"Cowardly old crows! Not one of them would even raise his voice to call us back. Not they! No, they drove the wagons for those damned gaugers, all the way to Hythe."

A silence, then Jacob Higgins said: "Got to say one thing, farmer—Lewis is learning his business. Good many years since a whole run was taken like that in this part of the world. A smart young man, like Lieutenant Finch of the *Harpy*, who killed Matt Prigg for me. And I tell you what, Bob: I'll set-tle with Finch, and if I can, I'll help you settle with Lewis."

"Settle is the word, Jacob; and now's the moment for it. If this were Hawkhurst now he'd get a bullet and no more argument about it. But I'm not a bloody cormorant like Toby Catt; we'll give him a taste of free traders' medicine and a trip to France. If the Frenchies string him up for a spy that's no concern of ours. He won't be the first gauger to fin-ish up kicking on a French rope."

They both laughed harshly, and Tom felt again the strange disturbance he'd felt the night he left. On the one hand, gaugers had to be punished and warned off if they harmed the trade, and carrying them to France and throw-ing them ashore there to take their chance was, he knew, a time-honored method in Kent and Sussex. On the other hand, he felt a sort of guilty relief that Lewis had shown himself not a craven but a cool and cunning enemy. He'd somehow lived up to what Tom had expected of him.

"But how the devil did he know, farmer? The time, the place, the way you work—everything!"

Gibbons's expression became savage, and he ran his eyes over the awed group of tubmen that stood listening. "How, Jacob? Why, a rat. A creeping, crawling hangdog spy! And if I knew the man—if I knew him and had him before me" —he raised his hands slowly, and the men cringed away— "then I'd twist the lousy life out of him with these, as soon as kill a fly." He stared passionately at each man in turn while the night seemed to hold its breath.

Higgins broke the tension. "Howsumdever, this Lewis— we'll try for him tonight, farmer, shall we? How do we nab him?"

"Well, I've only a few tubmen here tonight, for I didn't know whether you'd be here or not. They'll have to stow the tubs in my barn for the time being. But I've got all the batmen here, and by a bit of luck George has found the place where Lewis and his gaugers waited last night. You know the old sheep-fold just up the road, Tom? Well, he found all the grass trampled there, and fresh horsedroppings scattered about. Lewis is too sharp, you see, to try the same trick twice; he was going to jump on us as we were running the tubs ashore last night. Only, of course the tubs never came, so he slipped away, and now he doesn't know that we've twigged the place where he waited. Well, two can play at being cunning: I reckon he'll be there again later on tonight, ready for a two o'clock run. Only *this* time we'll be waiting for *him*. You'll come, Jacob, and see the fun? Tom, I want you, too. Time you learned how to deal with these tub-gauging vermin. He's no friend of yours, I know."

They went to where the six sinister black-faced batmen were waiting, and as they all walked up the road to the sheep-fold, Robert Gibbons fell in beside his son and laid an arm across his shoulders. "I'm sorry I gave you such a scurvy welcome, son. I've had my worries. Apart from the run being taken, I mean. Your mother, for a start, has been in a pretty state about you since last night. I've sent a man to the farm to let her know you're here safe and sound. And then . . . Mary has gone."

"Gone!" Tom felt a sudden horrible chill. He and his twin had never been parted before. "Where has she gone? And why?"

"Gone to Hastings as paid companion to some rich old hag of a widow. She'll not stand it long. The damned little baggage, she went without a by-your-leave; packed her traps into old Webb the carrier's cart and caught the Hastings coach at Rye, I suppose. Don't know what's amiss with her."

"I think I do, Father. I believe she was waiting that night for . . . for the dragoon——"

His father suddenly withdrew his arm and his voice grew harsh. "Hold your tongue, booby, if you don't want a hemp cravat! Didn't I tell you to wipe all that out of your mind? The silly puppy cut his own throat." He strode off into the darkness.

They reached the sheep-fold, stowed themselves in the low thorn bushes around it, put sticks and pistols at the ready, and settled to wait. Tom found it an eternity, crouching among the dry nettle stems, his legs becoming more and more cramped. An hour went by, its only sounds the screech of preying owls, the crackling of dry stems as men stirred, the monotonous champing and spitting of the tubman next to him, who was chewing a plug of run tobacco to calm his nerves. Tom felt taut all over; unlike his father, he didn't feel burning anger against Lewis, only the same kind of tension as he felt when, in the freezing January dawn, he crouched below the sea wall waiting for the "honk-honk" of the wild geese. Lewis wasn't the hated schoolmaster any more, but a quarry to be caught. He didn't think about what might follow.

Then, about midnight, the beat of horses' hoofs on the road and the sound of low voices. The sheep-fold was suddenly full of men on horseback; Tom thought he could make out five. Then he heard Lewis's voice, quiet, but full of authority: "Wait here, boys, while I go down to see what's stirring. Don't make a sound, but look to the priming of your pistols. I shall be back in ten minutes."

"Now, lads!" called Gibbons; the bushes crashed and crackled into life as the ambushers leaped out. There were cries of fear and astonishment from the gaugers, as each one of them saw the glint of a pistol leveled at his head, saw the grim black faces where only the whites of the eyes showed. In a few seconds it was all over; they were surrounded, helpless; the Customs House men knew well enough that with a Rye jury behind them the batmen would not hesitate to fire.

Gibbons's face showed up strangely white among the band. "Right, lads. So there we are! Tom, go round and collect their barkers, so there's no unpleasantness." Tom went quickly from man to man collecting the pistols; the Hythe men gave them up readily enough; their eyes bulged with terror, looking this way and that like cattle at a slaughter. Was this, they wondered, going to be settled Hawkhurst fashion with a bullet each and a rough grave on the marsh? Lewis looked long and contemptuously at Tom, without a trace of fear in his pale thin face, before handing over his guns without a word.

"That's better," said Gibbons. "Now, it's only Mr. Riding-officer Lewis we want. The rest of you lousy fat-gutted tub-gauging swine—use your spurs and get your dirty hides back where you belong—and think yourselves lucky we haven't let the daylight into 'em. But if we catch you here again, mind, it'll be a different tale." He flourished his horse-pistol. "Now shift—and don't stop!"

They did not need telling again; clattering on to the highway, they dug in their spurs and tore off at a full gallop, each man crouching low by his horse's neck in case of a farewell bullet. Silence fell again as the hoofbeats died away.

"Hold his horse's head, Tom," said Gibbons. "Now, Mr. Schoolmaster-cum-Welshman-cum-tub-gauger, a word with you!" At the last word, he leaped forward, seized the skirts of Lewis's coat, and hauled him crashing to the ground.

It was a short and brutal business. No amount of courage or fighting skill could help the Welshman now; he rolled helpless on the turf, his arms up over his head for protection, while the batmen beat him savagely, their shiny sticks rising and falling like smiths' hammers, thudding against his body and limbs. He made not a sound. Tom watched, fascinated and awed.

" 'Ere y'are, Mas'r Tom. You 'ave a goo! You owe 'im one or two," said one of the batmen, offering him his stick. At once Tom knew, from the feeling in his stomach, that he didn't want to, couldn't bring himself to do it.

The figure as their feet had stopped moving now. "Right. That'll do, boys," said Gibbons. "Had enough, Mr. Lewis? Like to tell us in Latin how you like it?" The batmen laughed brutally. Tom felt increasingly sick. "Now then, for your trip to France, sir. Got the rope, there? Truss him up and put him across his horse. Got his stateroom ready, Jacob?"

"Aye, ready enough. He can go in the forepeak, along with the paint and the tar and the cordage. We'll chuck him ashore at Dunkirk, and if the Frenchies jail him, shoot him, or hang him, well, it's all the same to me, I'm sure. If he ever does get back, farmer, you can depend upon it, he'll have learned his lesson tonight."

"Aye, we'll make a Tucker out of him yet—eh, Tom? My father broke him, years ago, and I'll be pleased to do the like for this one."

Tom saw Lewis only once during the voyage, when at noon the next day he was sent down with a seaman to take the Welshman a greasy dinner of salt beef hash. The lugger was running hard before a fresh westerly, rolling and laboring in the steep following sea. Right up in the bows there the motion was violent and sickening, so that even Tom, who was getting used to the sea, felt queasy. They pushed the hatch back, clumped down the ladder, and had to peer about in the damp evil-smelling hole before they saw him lying on an old sail. His face was deathly pale, except for a

77

great dark graze on one cheek-bone, his hands bruised and cut. He was asleep or unconscious when they came down. "'Ere, you, turn out and be damned," said the sailor, and would have kicked him in the ribs had not Tom pushed him roughly aside, saying quietly, "No! Enough's enough, for God's sake."

At the sound of the voices Lewis's eyes opened and he woke with an effort to his miserable plight. They watched him set his teeth and rise to a sitting position; after that beating, every movement must have been an agony to him, but again he made no sound. "Brought yer some lobscouse, gauger," said the sailor, with a good deal more respect in his voice.

Lewis looked straight ahead, his face set as granite: "I shall not eat it."

"Damn yer precious eyes—a lot we cares whether you eat it or not! Suit yerself, cully."

Lewis raised his eyes at the word "we," and looked long and straight at Tom. There was not a trace of any appeal for pity in that look, only dignity and a measureless contempt that seemed to pierce like a sword. Tom went up on deck hastily, shaken and wretched at the turmoil that was pulling him in half. The hard lump of gold in his money-belt brought to mind his father—his jollity, strength, bravery, handsome mastery—and the good things of the free trade—the adventure, the companionship, the harvest of gold, the excitement of cannon across a blue dancing sea. But the old ugly ghosts would stalk again—ghosts that seemed to cling to the trade: the torn body and tattered scarlet jacket of the young dragoon, old Henry Tucker galloping clownishly headlong to his death, the splash as Matt Prigg's body went in—and now Lewis.

9.   THE next evening, as the westerly fell light and the sky cleared, the *Two Brothers* ghosted with the last of the flood-tide up to her berth in Dunkirk Harbor. She thumped gently against the worn piles; the heaving-lines were caught by some fishermen, who grinned a welcome as they hauled up the mooring-ropes, and chatted in crude scraps of English and French. Duchamps came bustling across from his office in the warehouse, his arms waving, his fat red face split by a huge welcoming smile, crying out long before he reached them—"*M'sieur Gee-bon! M'sieur Eeg—inz!* Welcome back to Dunkerque. *Alors, un petit tot* in my office, *non?*"

Though this was his second trip as freighter, Tom was still bewildered and amused by the fantasy of it all—it was like something from the travels of Gulliver. Here they were, in the middle of a hostile port, yet not a shot had been fired at them—they had not even been stopped for searching. The name on their bow, the cut of their three lofty lugsails, had been enough for every guard-boat and shore-battery. And to-night the lugger's hands would be as free to walk about and drink in Dunkirk as they were in Rye—far freer, in fact, for in Rye they were in constant dread of the press-gang.

"Later on!" bawled back Higgins. "In a minute, Mr. Doo-shong. Got something to attend to first."

As soon as the wine merchant had gone, Higgins growled to a seaman, "Git him up here" and Lewis came clambering stiffly up from the forepeak, blinking his eyes in the late evening sunshine. He looked pale, sick and woebegone, as well as injured, yet though he looked a pitiful enough scarecrow he stood before the captain with the defiant indifference of a brave man condemned to death. His hat was gone, his hair tangled and wild, his Customs-House blue coat torn and dirty, but still recognizably a British uniform. He seemed to Tom like a man at point of death; how could he hope to survive dressed like that—homeless, friendless, penniless, in an enemy port?

Jacob Higgins mounted the short ladder on to the quay and looked round carefully. "Come up here, gauger," he called. "Now then, there's no soldiers nor gendarmes about —only sailors and such. I'm treating your fair, see, though I'm damned if you deserve it. I ain't giving you up to them. Clear out now, and whether they catch you and string you up, or you get away—'tis all one to me. But I tell you this: I shan't do this again. If you come back here, or interfere with a run of my goods again, it'll just be powder and lead and no argument. So sling your hook—and learn some sense while you're at it."

With the same air of quiet desperation Lewis turned on his heel without a word and walked off along the quay towards the town. Tom ran up the ladder out of morbid curiosity, and was just in time to see his blue-clad back disappear behind a line of drying nets. Higgins shook his head in grudging admiration. "Fine chap, young Tom. Blest if I could take it as quiet as that. Gawd knows if he'll ever see England again. Still," and he spat, "so much the better if he don't. If there's one customer I can't stomach, it's a gauger."

Before long the smuggler's crew were swilling their faces, combing out their wind-tangled hair and beards, and changing their tarry, greasy sea-going rig for smarter shore clothes, chattering excitedly like children at a treat. Nat Trotter, the ex-Navy gunner, gave a piercing whistle like that of a bosun's pipe, and bellowed: "Libertymen of the port watch, muster on the quarterdeck!" The others roared, and over the din Trotter cried to Tom: "Come on, then, my Tom! The brandy and the mamzelles are waiting! No quarter! A bottle and a wench apiece!"

All next day, with only two short breaks for meals, the work went on, the tiers of barrels rose and rose in the hold until Tom and the men working there had to bend double to avoid the deck-head beams. At last, late in the evening, a ragged cheer from the quay told them that the last barrel was on its way.

When darkness fell, Tom found himself alone aboard the lugger. Jacob had decided that he could spare the time for his hands to have another night ashore to make up for the weeks and weeks of continuous sea-time, but this time Tom had refused to go with them. He was exhausted by his day with the cargo, and still depressed by his nagging doubts. All this stealing, lying, cruelty, bloodshed—and for what? Gin and rum and brandy and tobacco and tea—no more than that. Could a man's life be valued in half-ankers? Were the tubs worth black holly-sticks raining down on a defenseless body? Or marooning a man where he was sure to be killed or jailed for life?

With these dreary ghosts tramping round in his brain he was beginning to doze off when he was jolted wide awake by the thump of feet on deck forward. One of the crew back early? No, this wasn't the blundering of a drunken sailor aboard his own ship, but the hesitant shuffle of a man being as quiet as he could. A thief, then! Higgins had asked him to look out for dockside pilferers—the place was notorious for them. "Take up my barker," he'd said, "and show 'em that. That'll make 'em scuttle!"

Tom was at home on the lugger now, and crept like a cat up the ladder, pistol cocked in his hand; he stood still, his heart pounding with excitement, as he reached the deck. Looking forward along the clean flush sweep of the lugger's deck, he could see, by the light of the wine shop across the quay, a dark shape hunched over the forepeak scuttle. He crept forward gingerly, placing every foot with care; 'twould be a pity, he decided, to shoo off this dockrat from here. Better to come close, give him a real fright, and perhaps a drubbing too. The feel of the heavy, polished pistol butt in his hand gave him a sense of strength and power. How the skulking wretch would jump!

What the devil was he doing, fumbling at the forepeak scuttle?

Near enough now!

"you!" He was surprised at the loudness of his own voice.

The bending man exploded in a gasp of surprise and fear, and faced about like a cat, instinctively raising his left arm to ward off a blow. The light from the tavern struck across his face—a white pointed face, with dark wide-staring eyes. Now Tom, too, was astonished.

"Lewis!"

The man lowered his arm. "Master Gibbons, I think?"

"Yes. What in God's name are you doing here?"

Lewis had mastered his surprise and panic now, and spoke quietly and calmly: "I knew this boat would be leaving for England soon. I assumed that everyone would be ashore swilling." Though he was still at the mercy of his enemies, his voice was hard, cold, cutting.

"But why *this* ship? Surely you——"

"Surely, Master Gibbons, there is no point in this conversation? Pull the trigger and have done with it. Settle it in your hearty Sussex free trader's fashion."

Tom flushed at the bitter jibe, flushed the more because he knew it was just. He gestured with the pistol, trying desperately to look as if he knew what to do. In fact, the only thing he knew was that he could not possibly bring himself to shoot Lewis in cold blood at point-blank range. "No!" he said, "I'm not a murderer. I am just ordering you to leave."

"And I am refusing to do so, so fire away, young man."

"Mr. Lewis, I am *ordering* you to go, or I'll——" Tom hesitated, hopelessly flustered. If a man ignored his pistol, what was left? He didn't wish to betray to Lewis how far he was on his side, but he had to say something. The raucous singing, shouting and screaming from the wine shop flowed across the quay into the silence between them. The shop door opened, then banged shut again as a fisherman lurched out.

Lewis still sat, immovable on the hatch-coaming. "You do not seem to see, young man, that the choice for me is not between life and death, but between a quick death and a slow one. If I go ashore I am like to be hunted down like a beast and hanged at the end of it. I came back here hoping to get away. I have failed as a fugitive, just as I failed as an exciseman. Very well, I sit here until you blow my brains out; if you cannot or will not do it, I shall wait here for your free trading friends. I have no doubt they will."

"No, sir, please don't wait for them!"

Lewis looked up sharply at the "sir" and at the new tone in the voice. Could his sworn enemy Tom Gibbons be a weak link? He began again warily: "Very well, then—there is another way. Help me to stow away and land in Sussex, and I swear that no man shall ever know that you played a part in it."

"My father would——"

"Your father need never know. It is for you to choose. But depend upon it, I will not be hunted like a rat."

A long pause. Tom bit his lip in the torment of deciding. "I'll do it," he said at last.

"And I will swear to secrecy. My hand upon it." He held out his right hand, and found it clenched with more warmth than he had expected. "Ahhh! Gently, young man, gently! It is still somewhat tender. No matter—it saved my head!"

Tom felt a horrible shame on being reminded of the beating. God knew he had hated and despised the Welshman enough in the past, yet there was this curious bond of respect and loyalty for the man who had taught him Virgil. The words were forced out of him: "I didn't . . ."

"No. I shouldn't expect it of you." And Lewis smiled—his first smile for many a day.

Tom looked anxiously over his shoulder at the brawling wine shop. At any moment the whole crew might erupt and come reeling back, drunk enough for any violence or cruelty to the hated gauger. "Now you must get out of sight, sir," he said. "Where are you going to hide?"

"I am no sailor, Tom, as you know. I know only the part of the ship where I was . . . entertained, shall we say? What do you say to the forepeak? They would surely not think of looking there?"

Tom considered for a moment, then shook his head: "No, that won't do. There are all kinds of stores and sails there. Someone might come down there at any time. I can't think of anywhere that is safe."

"I have another suggestion: I noticed on the voyage over

that there is a kind of hatch secured by bolts in the front wall——"

"For'ard bulkhead."

Lewis smiled. "You are an apt pupil, Tom, as I have always known. The for'ard bulkhead, then, of the forepeak. Now, what is behind that hatch?"

"The cable-locker—where the anchor-chain lies when the anchor is up on deck."

"Does the cable occupy the whole space?"

"Oh no, not half of it."

"Very well, then. I will camp on top of the cable. With an old sail I shall do well enough."

Tom went white. "No! For God's sake, Mr. Lewis, not in the cable-locker! You don't understand!"

"I understand well enough," said Lewis impatiently, "that I must find somewhere—and that soon."

"Aye, but not there! If Jacob Higgins let go an anchor while you were in there you'd be a dead man in a second. I know. The anchor must weigh four hundredweight . . . the chain would catch round your limbs . . . you'd be . . . It happened in Rye once—when I was a small boy. A man had stowed away aboard a collier brig; he was in the locker when she let go . . . They say he was . . ."

"You may spare me the details, Tom." Lewis pointed at him in his schoolmasterly way. "Now then, let us look at this problem like philosophers, as I have taught you: you do not approve the cable-locker?"

"No."

"Because if we let go anchor I shall be a dead man?"

"Yes."

"Good. Now, in the *normal* course of the voyage, *will* he let go the anchor?"

"No. But there might——"

"Wait! No 'mights.' I said the 'normal' course. Now then,

85

are there any other compartments in this ship big enough to hide me, where no sailor will ever come?"

"Well . . . No." The answer was reluctant, dragged out of him.

"And if I were discovered?"

"They would kill you."

"Exactly. So that in a normal voyage I shall probably be safe in the locker, and dead anywhere else. Quod erat demonstrandum."

Tom looked at him silently, thinking—if it were me, I would sooner face Higgins than lie two or three days in that filthy pitch-black hole, not knowing the moment when the loops and coils of heavy chain may go roaring out of the navel-pipe above you, pulling you to pieces in the process. Quod erat demonstrandum is all very well about triangles in a schoolroom, but a man has nerves too.

Lewis looked in his turn at Tom, remembering a remark of Lord Tillingham's: "The boy looks and acts just like his gamecock of a father, but they say he follows his mother too. Sensible woman, Mrs. Gibbons—shrewd and gentle. Gibbons needs a wife like that!"

Then they busied themselves: Lewis opened the hatch in the forepeak and climbed on to the random, deadly heap of chain in the locker. The stench in that airless hole was appalling, for every time the cable was hove up it brought stinking black mud up with it, which in time dried and powdered off on to the bottom of the locker. Tom passed him in an old headsail for a bed, then he found an empty half-anker tub and filled it with water. Raking about in the galley, he found biscuit and scraps of meat which he thought would not be missed. As they worked, they talked; Lewis told him how he had spent the day aboard a Genoese merchantman. The crew had been friendly, and had fed him well; he had even been able to talk to them, for they half-understood his Latin. He could have sailed with them. "But they were chartered and loaded for Madagascar and Batavia, Tom, and I had no mind to spend a year roaming the tropics. I have a father and mother too, in Merthyr."

They arranged the future as best they could. If all went well, Tom was to slip below as they closed the coast, undo the bolts and allow Lewis out before the anchors went down. They hoped that by then all hands would be on deck and too busy with ship-handling to go below. Lewis was to hide in the forepeak, however, until the boat was away and the tow-line paying out. If the worst happened, and Jacob decided for some reason to anchor on the way, Tom was to get him out, and he would take his chance hiding in the forepeak.

Lewis's last words, as the imprisoning hatch closed on him, were solemn: "I'm utterly in your hands now, Tom. We may be on opposite sides, but somehow I feel I would trust no man more. One day, perhaps, I can repay you."

Then the hatch was shut, and the Welshman was alone in his terrible sanctuary—or grave.

Tom spent the rest of the next afternoon and evening in a misery of suspense and indecision. The trouble was that they had time to waste before going in to Camber Beach, and twice he heard men mention the possibility of anchoring inshore somewhere where it was lonely. Thus Tom had to stay on deck all the time in case they did. Lewis would just have to pile out and hope for the best. Tom found himself obsessed by the little hole in the deck, the navel-pipe, by which the cable passed in and out of the locker, and kept wondering how the poor devil was managing. The motion in there, for one thing, would be sickening. He was afraid someone would notice the way he was hanging about there forward. As it was, Jacob had been very suspicious about the pistol, which he had forgotten to replace in the cabin; Tom had had to invent a night intruder whom he'd frightened off. He had a feeling that Higgins was not altogether satisfied with this fiction, though.

Luckily, it was pitch dark when they at last closed the coast, and all the hands were standing by the halyards or getting the tubs tied to the tow-line. No one noticed him drifting towards the forepeak or diving suddenly into it. He crouched at the hatch, listening intently in case anyone was following. Then he drew the bolts and opened up the hatch; at once he heard Lewis stir on the clinking chain. He had to help him out, for the Welshman could scarcely move for cramp. "Are you well, Mr. Lewis?" he whispered.

"I'm alive, Tom. Sick as a dog and devilishly cramped, but alive. Are we there? Good. Now, go to the stern of the boat and leave the rest to me. Then, if I am caught—well, you have naught to do with it. Good-bye, Tom, and thank you from my heart!" They gripped hands again briefly; Tom slithered out of the forepeak unnoticed in the bustle and went aft. He knew it would be fatal if anyone noticed him continually glancing forward, so he resolutely turned his back and lent a hand with the urgent work of swinging up the tubs.

It was three hours before he could sneak below again; he called softly, but there was no reply. Lewis was gone. How would a sick, spent, cramped man, still grievously bruised from his beating, manage a half-mile swim in the cold breakers? *He* will manage it, Tom thought, if that is what he has decided. He is not a man to fail at things. But where do *I* stand? Am I gauger or free trader, a King's man or an outlaw, a good son or a family traitor?

10. THOMAS CAPPER, butler to Lord Tillingham, had had a bad fright. His bare feet flapped as he labored up the stairs, gathering his flannel nightshirt to his knees; he gasped and whimpered to himself as he ran panting along the corridor; the marble floor froze his feet, but he hardly noticed. In thirty years at Tillingham Place he'd seen and heard many strange things and not turned a hair—but a man back from the dead! A man talking and walking, but as wet, dirty and pale as if he had been newly dug out of the clay. One look had been enough! The feeble tapping at the door in the middle of the night—the yawning, stretching and unbarring! And then the Thing, falling in at his feet! He had had to run to someone stronger, someone who would know what to do.

Tap, tap at the door.

But what would *he* say at being awakened three hours before dawn?

Tap, tap.

No sound from within. The last time he'd done this was the night the Great Tide had flooded half of Rye.

Tap, tap.

And then there had been the night twenty years ago—

when the horseman had ridden over from Folkestone to say that Lady Tillingham had died in giving birth to Master Humphrey.

He knocked a fourth time, louder now, for he was becoming desperate. "Yes?" A sleepy voice from within. Then, as Capper entered, and the sleeper realized the monstrous hour, the voice became angry: "What in the name of . . . What the devil do you mean, sir, by rousing me at this hour?"

"My lord, your pardon . . . I beg your p——"

"What is it, Capper?"

"It's . . . it's the Welshman, sir . . ."

Lord Tillingham sat up sharply: "What? Have they found his body? Or his murderers?"

"No, sir, no. He's not . . . he's . . . here!"

"Here? *Alive?* Mr. Lewis—*alive?*"

"My lord, I don't know what——" Capper stopped, for his master had snatched his candle and was now half way to the head of the stairs.

By the time he reached the bottom, Iorwerth Lewis, half dead from exhaustion, his face still dark with bruises, his clothes wet from the sea, and plastered with mud from walking across ploughed fields, had raised himself from the floor where Capper had left him, and was lying back in a chair. His head had fallen right back, his throat showing a gleaming white in the candlelight.

Lord Tillingham stopped, shocked into silence. "Dear God," he whispered at last, "what have they done to him?" And then, rousing himself to action: "Capper, take his legs. Help me to put him on my couch in the library. There is still some fire in there."

"But, sir, his clothes . . . the dirt and the wet . . . the covers will be ruined."

"*Capper!*" The butler jumped at the voice, and together

90

they laid Lewis out comfortably. Capper ran to and fro, fetching clean dry clothes and blankets, food and brandy. They forced the liquor between his teeth and waited for life to return. The nobleman meanwhile glared across the unconscious form at his servant, and his words were ominously calm: "Now then, Capper, a word in your ear: Mr. Lewis is back; he will not be going off my estate for some time. No one knows that he is here, apart from you and me. Naturally, the other servants will have to know. But, my friend, no one else must hear of it. *No one!* You understand? I want you to tell them all in the morning that if any word leaks out before I give leave I will send the whole tribe of you packing—men, women, boys, girls! The whole tribe. And I will have you whipped before I discharge you, Capper. So think well before you begin gossiping. Digging ditches will come hard to you after the soft life you have of it here, eating my pheasant and drinking my burgundy."

Capper flushed at the sharp words. The Welshman's eyelids began to flutter. Capper was dismissed. "I will tend him now. Get to bed, Capper—and no keyholes. The hall is draughty—you will catch an ague out there."

Lewis opened his eyes at the sound of the door closing; he smiled weakly and spoke in a low voice: "My lord! I am back, you see. Thank you for your nursing."

"It is nothing—it was I who allowed you to become riding-officer. We had given you up for dead, Iorwerth. I have already written to the Commissioners of Customs acquainting them with your disappearance."

"They were merciful this time, my lord, the free traders. Not death. Only a cruise to Dunkirk and back." Lewis smiled bitterly. "The outward journey in a paint-store, the return one in the cable-locker."

Lord Tillingham frowned and whistled low in astonishment. "The cable-locker? But you——" Then he checked himself. "But I am being a poor nurse. Rest is what you need, my friend; rest and quiet. I will see that you get it. You must tell me your adventures after you have slept. Eat a little of this cold fowl now, if you wish, and then rest. You are among friends now."

Amidst his pain and exhaustion, Lewis felt a little glow of pleasure and pride. Lord Tillingham had used his Christian name for the first time.

The late dusk was falling next day when Lewis, having nearly slept the clock round, walked slowly and stiffly between the lofty elms of the North Walk with Lord Tillingham. It was a perfect evening in early summer, the mists and the earth-smells rising in the chilly air, a robin and a blackbird singing their last songs of the day, owls beginning their soft, deadly flights.

"I see," the nobleman was saying. "So Tom Gibbons, of all people, came to your rescue. I should not have thought it. Men are strange creatures."

"He was not inclined to at first," said Lewis smiling. "My heart stopped for fear when I saw him there with his confounded barker. But, poor lad, I'm afraid I gave him little choice. In the heat of a fight, with a dozen smugglers round him, he might perhaps have blazed away. But how could he when he and I were alone, and as close as you and I are now?"

"Quite so. But he is, as I think I told you, several shades more civilized and reasonable than his father. I hear, by the by, that his sister has left home lately . . . but if Robert Gibbons should ever learn——"

"Yes, I too am concerned about that. He would be beside himself. But he shall never find out from me. I have sworn that."

92

"And very right too. Well, what are your own plans now? I and the other Commissioners will quite understand if, in view of your rather scurvy introduction to the excise service, and your dastardly betrayal by the Customs House men, you should decide to return to your books. No man will blame you."

"Resign? No, my lord! Of course, if you choose to dismiss me for incompetence——"

"Soft, soft, my touchy young friend! We have not the slightest intention of doing that."

"Very well, then; I wish to continue until I have reduced the barbarity and anarchy that has gone on so long. As for my men—do not be hard on them. They are ordinary men. It was my own folly which led them into the trap. I have learned my lesson—never do the same thing or go to the same place twice running."

Still talking, they left the gravel drive and, passing through a small gate, entered a large meadow. At their approach, the herd of red Sussex cattle which had been browsing under the trees at the far end lifted their heads and began to trot towards them, kicking up their back heels in sheer high spirits until the clods flew. Lewis, the townsman, started in fear and caught the nobleman by the arm, pointing at the massive young bull that swung along at their head: "My lord—a bull—should we not . . . ?"

Lord Tillingham laughed easily. "You're a strange fellow, Iorwerth, to fear my little beauty here more than you do a gang of cut-throat cormorants. Never fear, I walk here every night. I'll answer for his manners."

Sure enough, the bull stopped and gazed at them amiably, twitching his ears and tail against the flies. Still, Lewis looked carefully at the long cruel sweep of his horns, thin and curved like a scimitar, their points black and sharp.

"Allow me to introduce the apple of my eye. Tillingham

Cœur-de-Lion is his name officially, though I confess that Jem, my herdsman, always calls him Old Tup, and I have caught the habit."

"I'm glad to make his acquaintance, by any name he wishes. And I say very sincerely that I hope he will always look upon me as a friend!"

Lord Tillingham, smiling, had gone right up to the bull, stroking its nose affectionately. "To you he may be no more than a danger, but to me he represents twenty years of work and breeding. Look at that fine male head held high, the deep shoulders, the barrel chest, those round rumps of his. His sons and daughters will help to put good blood into half the herds in Sussex, if my plans come to pass."

They left the herd and walked back to the house, whose windows now gleamed with lamplight. Lord Tillingham spoke gravely as they walked: "You spoke just now of your incompetence, but it is I who have failed. Miserably. For twenty years, since my wife died, I have shut myself up and buried my head in State papers, trying to right things in London or Scotland or Canada or India, and all the time the most monstrous misrule has gone on outside my own park gates—the law defied and made a farce, armed gangs riding about, sometimes even in daylight; men corrupted, juries bribed, innocent villagers beaten, terrified into silence, killed . . . And we have all jested about it, and said 'The smuggler—oh, a rogue, to be sure, but a good honest one!' Well, it must stop, and I will do what I can to see that it does, at least in my own corner of Sussex."

"The worst difficulty, my lord, is the Sussex juryman. I can bring as many men as I please to trial, but I am told on all hands that they will go scot-free and laughing."

"Aye. But there are ways and means, Iorwerth, ways and means. Do you catch me a free trader or two, and I will do the rest."

11. Two weeks and two uneventful voyages after Lewis's nightmare return, Tom Gibbons sat hunched on the forward end of the forehatch of the *Two Brothers*, staring into the white nothingness of a sea fog. The warm south-easter on their port beam seemed to be sucking the vapor up out of the sea in rising wisps that formed into rolling, stifling wet woolly blankets of fog. Sometimes the lugger would come out into a narrow lane between banks, where a weak-looking but warm sun tinted the crinkled sea blue; then she would plunge into another roll of fog, the warmth would disappear, the sea become lifeless and leaden again. The fog distilled on every sail, rope and spar, and ran in even drops, which fell in showers whenever the breeze lifted or shook the canvas.

An hour ago, off Dover, they had been in the midst of the shipping, and the noises of bells, horns and voices had come eerily out of the void around them. Tom had gone forward as an extra lookout, but by now his mind was miles away, wondering about Iorwerth Lewis, the man he ought to hate but could not. Higgins's men, and his father's men too, all talked about him as if he were dead, or as good as dead. Not a word had been said in Camber about his return, which was surprising if he was in the same house as Master Capper. But *had* he returned? That was the question depressing Tom. Had all the plotting and worrying, all that incredible calm courage been in vain? He had certainly gone over the side that night, but half a mile of cold water was a long swim for a man in his state. Perhaps after all that suffering and trying his lifeless body was swilling to and fro, east and west, in the ebb and flow of the Channel tides.

There was something else on Tom's mind that morning —nothing definite, but a foreboding certainty that something was in the wind. Why the different course, for instance? Instead of keeping to the French side (safer for them than the English), Jacob Higgins had struck across the Straits for Dover, and now he was slipping along the edge of Dymchurch Sands, dangerously close inshore in only three fathoms of water. In fact, the only noise on deck was the regular plunge of the leadline and the quiet monotonous calls of the leadsman: "By the mark, three . . . Deep four . . . And a half three!" It was all very queer; why creep along the sand like this, and risk a stranding, when the straight course kept you in deep water? And, even stranger, why had the muskets and cutlasses been brought out and put ready? The hands knew something was afoot, for instead of keeping to their sea-routine of scrubbing, splicing, painting, tarring and greasing, they stood about in groups, muttering and pointing. Higgins himself alternately gazed intently ahead and paced about, chafing. When some men laughed aloud, he silenced them savagely. "Stow yer gab, you stupid braying idjuts!" Ever since the voyage with Lewis, Tom had been living his life mechanically, dully—"like a damned sleep-walking booby" was his father's phrase for it; now at last he felt his interest quicken.

96

He rose and went over the foremast shrouds, where stood the fat ungainly figure of Peter Smallman, the lugger's cook. He had come up for a breather from the stifling air of his little galley, and stood there blowing and gasping, wiping the sweat from his face and neck.

"What is happening this morning?"

"Cook, I am, Master Gibbons, not cap'n. Ask Jacob."

"He seems to be looking for something. But why is he in so close?"

"Well, 'tis foggy, see. The forts can't see him. As for what he's looking for," he closed an eye in a cunning wink, "maybe it's to do with the *Harpy*, what gave us such a drubbing."

"*Harpy*? He won't want to meet *her*, surely?"

"No. But they say she's anchored off Folkestone."

"Then why . . . ?"

"P'raps it might be the guard-boat from her. P'raps Jacob's heard that she's providing the rowing-guard along Dymchurch Sands this week."

"I see." Tom knew about the rowing guard-boat; you could see one most days from Camber Beach—a small galley manned by Customs House men which was intended to stop small-scale smuggling by fishing-boats. The guard-boat always took the greatest care not to meddle with an armed, heavily-manned lugger like the *Two Brothers*. They left her to the Revenue cutter and her six-pounders.

"But," Tom said, still puzzled, "they won't interfere with us. I still don't see . . ."

Smallman leaned closer and breathed in his ear: "P'raps they won't. But p'raps Jacob wants to interfere with *them*. They're from the *Harpy*, y'see. He ain't forgot the pounding he got from her, when young Prigg got spiked. He ain't a forgiving man, Jacob."

"You don't mean he'd deliberately attack a boat-load of helpless men?"

"I don't know, master. Like enough he won't find them in this murk. But if he does . . . well, I'd as soon not be in the boat, that's all—Hey! Ain't that summat out there ahead?" He turned, waved to catch the skipper's eye, and pointed into the fog dead ahead. Yes, there was something! A dark smudge, which became more distinct as they watched—a form like a huge black water-beetle ambling lazily across the smooth-rolling surface. They had come up dead astern of the guard-boat, which was loitering along carelessly and noisily on her dull and endless patrol. The fierce, silent men of the lugger heard the sound of the excisemen's chattering and guffawing as they drew nearer.

Now they could make out three oars on each side, and a knot of four men sprawled in the stern-sheets, eating, drinking and smoking. So negligent was their watch that they had not seen the big lugger even now. Only ten men, off their guard, their muskets probably unprimed and wet with fog. It would not be a long battle.

Then at last Tom could tell that they had been seen. There was a quick stifled shout and a babel of arguing, while the oarsmen rested on their oars. Then a rather quavering hail: "What ship is that?" It sounded as if the speaker knew the answer only too well.

There was a pause while the boat waited, heaving gently up and down, and the tall, shark-like shape slid yet nearer; then Higgins called in a clear voice: "*Two Brothers*, lugger, of Rye."

The reply caused a hustle of urgent, whispered debate among the excisemen. Then, the three port oars threshed the water, the boat swung round to starboard and all the rowers bent their backs, dug in their blades and began to pull for dear life to get to shallow water where the deep-hulled lugger could not follow. It was a good move on their part, but for a while it left their whole broadside exposed to the smugglers.

"Nat," said Jacob to his best marksman, "plug me one of the midship oars." The Customs men saw the long thin barrel leveled at them, and a man in the stern—the coxswain, perhaps, leaped up, waving his arms and calling in a shrill, terrified voice: "No, Captain, no, no! For Christ's sake, Captain, don't fire! You can proceed . . . we're not going to search you!"

Crack! The gun flashed bright in the gray fog. Nat could not miss at the range. The midship oarsman on the starboard side gave a croak and flopped forward over the loom of his oar; this one shot so jammed the oars on the starboard side that in a moment the boat was stopped again, swinging slowly round to face the towering bows of the lugger, which still slid remorselessly on. There was an agonized second, in which the poor wretches in the boat realized fully at last what Jacob Higgins intended. Two of them were in the act of loading their neglected muskets when the lugger hit the bow of the boat with a grinding, splintering crash, pushed it bodily round until it was broadside on, then ground steadily over it, fragments like matchwood bobbing up on both sides. Like most sailors of their day the excisemen could not swim. Until the last moment they stayed in the security of their boat; then, as it heeled and filled, and began to break up with tearing, rending groans, they jumped this way and that, giving brief screams of terror which the deadly water choked in their throats. Surprised, terrified, hampered by coats and seaboots, a mile off shore, they floundered and threshed in the water, and the smugglers, silent so long, roared and cackled at them in delight and triumph, jeering and shouting advice at the dying men.

Till now, Tom had watched in a kind of dream, unable to believe what he was seeing. Now, sick and full of rage at the same time, he tore aft to where Higgins stood by the helmsman, and thrust his face at the smiling skipper. "When are you going to stop?"

"Stop? What for, young farmer?" said Higgins casually.

"What for? To pick up those men, of course!"

"Pick 'em up, Master Gibbons? What do I want with 'em?"

"They're men—they're drowning!"

"Drowning, yes. As for men—well, I don't know about that. They look like gaugers to us." The reply brought a thick laugh from the hands who had left the side to watch the scene between their skipper and this strutting young upstart.

Tom was wide-eyed and desperate. "You're a murderer if you leave them."

Higgins's smile died suddenly. "Oh yes? And what was they when they killed Matt Prigg? I said then I'd pay *Harpy* out, and I have. That's very-near half her crew."

Tom was beyond all control. "You *must*! I order you to stop!"

Higgins's only reply was to spit contemptuously over the side. In an instant, Tom leaped forward, gave the helmsman a push in the chest that jolted him sprawling into the scuppers, and thrust with all his weight on the tiller to bring the ship up into the wind. She heeled at this rough treatment, her gear began to shake, raining down waterdrops from the sails, but before she came head to wind, Tom felt an iron hand seize his arm, and he ducked his head to a tremendous blow from Higgins's other fist. He was catapulted from the tiller up against the stolid ring of seamen that stood around. Out of the corner of his eye he saw the dull gleam of a musket-barrel; with a savage wrench he tore it from the

100

man's grasp, and he would have aimed and fired at Higgins with it if the gun had not been snatched again by someone with twice his strength. He heard the voice of Smallman the cook murmuring in his ear: "Don't wave that about, my son. Don't try it. He'd have his dirk in your guts before you could aim it. Leave go, mate."

Then his blind rage turned to an almost weeping despair. He shook free and looked wildly this way and that at them all. "You're bloody cowardly murderers—all of you!" he shouted.

The tension was over; they roared and shouted with laughter at him. "Nat," said Higgins, "what's he on about? I ain't sure."

"Summat about picking up gaugers, I believe, skipper."

"Gaugers? What gaugers?" Jacob shaded his eyes, looking all around him at the fog. "I can't see no gaugers!"

It was true. Astern, there was now no sound, nor anything in sight but the wreathing fog. Somewhere in their wake one or two cold and exhausted men might be clinging to the wreckage of the boat, but that, too, was in the grip of the tide, and in an hour's time it would be off Dungeness Point, being drawn into the white wide wastes of the Channel, beyond all hope of rescue.

"You," said Higgins, "what reckon you can give orders: I'll learn you who's captain here. Lucky for you your dad's a friend of mine, Gawd help him. If you was in my crew I'd flog you till I could see yer backbone. Git out o' my sight down the forepeak where we put that damned gauger chap. Seems to me you're more on his side than what you are on ours. And you can tell your dad when you see him that you've had your last trip aboard the *Two Brothers*."

12. OLD Seth Hewett, the verger, limped across the transept to the north door, finding his way surely through the gathering shadows in the church. He turned the big key in the lock, and then froze in a spasm of terrible fear, for he heard his name spoken quietly, and there was the dead man Lewis sitting motionless in a pew, not six feet away, his queer pointed face all pale, his eyes dark pits, just as he was alive!

The old man choked and clung to a pew-end for support. His voice was low, broken, earnest: "You! You've come back to . . . to see me! Dear God, I never did you no harm . . . 'Twasn't me as told 'em where to find you . . . May I be struck dead if I gave you away . . . Our . . . our Father, 'chart in Heaven——"

He broke off with a sob as the ghost stood up and moved along the pew to approach him; it spoke again: "Mr. Hewett, it does you credit to say your prayers, but there is really no need on my account. As you see, I am not dead, and never have been dead. Half dead—yes, on several occasions, but dead—no! Now, take my hand, sir, and you will find it warm flesh and blood. Pray, don't draw away—I shall not eat you!"

102

Their hands met and clasped, but the old man had been so shocked that it was several minutes before he could be persuaded that Lewis was a man, not a ghost. At last, however, they fell to talking in their old businesslike way, and the verger's spirits began to rise at the thought that after all there might still be more profit to be made. "When will there be another run?" asked Lewis.

"There's one tonight, sir."

"H'm . . . too late to arrange anything for that. And the next?"

"What's today? Friday . . . that means . . . we'll say next Wednesday, I should think. I'll know by Monday, I lay. See you in here Monday night."

"Very well. Now, no one must know that I am alive and on duty again. You understand? No one. We may be able to spring another surprise."

The old man shook his head. "You don't want to count on that, sir. Since that night at Guldeford Corner they've been guarding the goods with armed men even after they're in the wagons."

"I see. But the guards must be dismissed at some time?"

"Not till they unload; they got to see it safely to where it's going. That's Farmer Gibbons's orders now. They got to see the goods off the street and into a store. Then they can go and get their guinea each."

"I see. Now, where are the goods finally unloaded?"

"All over the place, sir. The Red Lion, Hawkhurst, is a fav'rite place—and Booth the grocer—he's got a good big old cellar. But there's half-a-dozen other places—farms and inns mostly—that they use."

"I should like to know where Wednesday's run is going."

"Ah, sir!" The old man was thoroughly back to normal; he winked with an air of greedy cunning. "That's harder to find out, that is. I got to ask more questions, take more of a chance. That'll cost you more than——"

"It will not cost me a penny more than we have agreed, Hewett," said Lewis crisply. "You will find out what I wish to know by Monday or you will not get a guinea more from me."

Breakfast at Peasmarsh Farm was a gloomy affair next morning. The lovely long sunny farm kitchen was the same as ever; so were the solid table, the plentiful farm food, the ash sticks crackling quietly in the stove, the three cats serenely washing their faces and ears after a night's mousing round the stacks, the blue Dutch china displayed on the dresser. But instead of a cheerful chattering family round the table there were just two people, each of whom was shut up in the torment of private thoughts.

At one end of the table, Robert Gibbons, who had not long come back from his night's work, was cramming his mouth with boiled ham in a kind of silent savagery. By God, that boy was going to feel his right arm when he showed his face again. And where the devil had the fool sloped off to? Not been in all night; how dare he worry Ethel like that? He stole a furtive glance at her. She was sipping tea, and trying to keep calm, but he could see her cup trembling, and her eyes red with crying. It was so rare for her to cry that he felt softened, ashamed of his black mood. "Come, don't look so downcast, Ethel," he said. "He'll be back soon. I'll deal with the booby, and teach him not to make you worry like this. Then it will all be over and done with."

Far from comforting her, his words made her shake her head despairingly, dislodging a tear. "You don't understand, Robert. You don't begin to understand your own children. You've lost us Mary, and now you'll lose Tom."

104

Gibbons's anger reawoke. "Stuff and nonsense, woman. I know the lad. I'll clip his wings for him. When I say 'come' he comes. As for Mary—that was different. She's a woman; I never have known how to deal with women. Queer creatures, females."

Ethel Gibbons swallowed and seemed to gather courage for what she was going to say. "At all events, Robert, you don't deal with a girl by shooting her young man."

There was a second's utter silence, then Gibbons threw down his knife and fork and leaped up, throwing the chair over backwards. Black as thunder with rage, he turned to storm out of the house, but he had scarcely taken a step when there was a click from the latch of the back door, and there was Tom, dark and tall against the morning sun that came streaming in. "Aha," said the farmer. "You! Where have you been, sirrah? Out all night when I needed you, coming back like a hangdog cur, looking as if you'd slept in a hedge."

Ethel Gibbons ran to him and embraced him, sobbing. "Tom, where have you been all night? Your clothes—they're all wet!"

"I've been walking around the lanes. I met old Mother Fagg. She gave me some breakfast."

"Very well, woman, very well! Let me deal with him," said Robert. "A man might think he was a long-lost prodigal, instead of a clown due for a whipping. Now, sir, the gun-room, at once!"

Tom stared impassively at his father and walked away to the gun-room without a word. Ethel caught her husband's arm as he went to follow. "Now Robert, please, *please* don't be too hard! He's our only boy, and he *is* only a boy! Remember what I said——"

"Enough, woman! Do I try to teach you how to sew and

105

bake? Don't tell me how to manage my own son. I'll deal with him as I deal with a horse who won't work—thrash him!"

The gun-room was unlike any other room in the house, for it was the only one which Ethel Gibbons and the maids never entered. Robert Gibbons used it as an office for his farm and free trading accounts, so that the old table in it was littered with papers and old worn-out quills. There were a few chairs, but nowhere to sit down, for all of them were taken up by a vast assortment of sporting gear and rubbish—kegs of powder, ramrods, bundles of wadding, powder-horns, bags of bullets and shot, fishing-rods, harness and saddles. A fox's mask grinned bitterly from the wall, and on the window-sill was a moth-eaten and balding stuffed weasel. When the two men walked in, the dust rose and danced in the sunbeams; the tiny moths whirled wildly as Gibbons shut the door with a tremendous bang. Underneath his fury he was beginning almost to enjoy his feeling of righteous indignation. The boy would have to come to heel and be taught what it was to disobey a father.

"Now, sir," said Gibbons, picking up a riding-crop and tapping his left palm with it, "you will be good enough to explain your conduct to Jacob Higgins and to me. You have so disgraced yourself at sea that Jacob says—and I do not blame him—that he will not have you aboard again. Then, just when I needed you badly, you must needs go wandering off like a diddecoy. By God. Tom, you owe us both an apology—when I've done with you. Do you not, now?"

The boy flushed, and shrugged sullenly. "I don't know."

"Don't know? Jackanapes! I'd better teach you, then." And he grasped the boy's sleeve with his left hand while his right began to raise the crop. He was surprised when Tom shook off his grasp and backed away.

"No, Father, wait! I can't beg your pardon—or Jacob

Higgins's—for I don't feel sorry for what I've done. I would do it again. And, Father, I will not be beaten for it. I'm not a little boy who has torn his breeches or teased the cat."

"Not a boy? No, you're worse than that—you're an insolent base ungrateful jackass!"

"Say what you like, I'd rather be a fool than a murderer. You weren't aboard that lugger off Dymchurch. You didn't see what Higgins did. You didn't hear them screaming, or see them dying."

Gibbons sobered and softened. How could he rage at the boy when he too felt that Jacob had gone too far, been needlessly cruel? "Aye, that . . . Well, I'll be frank with you: I don't like it either. 'Twasn't necessary or right."

"But don't you see, Father, that it is the sort of thing which continually happens in this so-called free trade? And what Mr. Lewis said about free traders acting as spies' messengers for the French is true—at least Higgins is one."

"What do you know about it? I don't believe it!"

"Father, nearly every time I've been to Dunkirk an official French government messenger has come aboard. I've seen him and Jacob exchanging oilskin envelopes. What could they have been if they were not messages to agents in England?"

"Rubbish, rubbish—could have been anything. And I don't like the way you say 'so-called' free trade! I'm being as patient as I can, but don't presume upon it. 'Free trade' was a good enough name for your grandfather and great-grandfather."

"Well, whatever the name, it is the same bloody business. Think of it, Father—what has happened since I began to take a hand in it: the dragoon—you frown, but it is no use to pretend that he is not dead at our hands—then there was old Henry Tucker, and now this—a whole boat's crew, in cold blood." He paused. "And there was Mr. Lewis, too."

"Lewis? That damned, canting, interfering Taffy! By God, this is too much, sir! Don't tell me you're sorry for *him* now? This is gratitude indeed! After the way he treated you, and the way I backed you up! Got the rascal turned away. I'm damned if I begin to understand you."

"It is quite simple, Father: once I would have liked to beat him senseless with these—he held up his big strong hands—"but it made me sick to see one man pulled down and beaten half dead with swinglers by half a dozen."

"Tchah! He was a gauger. Nothing's too bad for them. And you can save your pity for the fellow, for like enough the Frenchies have caught him and strung him up by now!"

"You'll soon see whether——" Tom stopped suddenly, biting his lower lip. His anger had nearly made his tongue run away with him. In another second the whole story would have been out. Luckily his father was now so furious that he did not notice the slip. He brought the riding-crop down on the table with a vicious crack.

"Silence! Enough of this whining rubbish! When I was your age I would not have dared to stand up and argue with my father in this way. You have defied me and disgraced me in the eyes of my friend, and you are going to suffer for it whether you like it or not. After that, you can turn out and pull your weight with the rest next Wednesday night, and we'll say no more about it. Now turn round, sir, and bend over."

"No, Father, I will not! I will not do any more smuggling for you, nor will I be beaten like a child. I am old enough to have a mind of my own——"

He got no further, for his father, now scarlet with rage, lashed out at him with the crop, and caught him full across his left cheek, just as the dragoon had caught Toby Catt. Tom gave a loud cry of pain, but, far from cowing him, the blow made him as furious as his father; he leaped forward as his father was raising the crop for a second blow, seized his right wrist with one hand, and, with the other, wrenched the crop away before his father had recovered from the surprise. For an instant it looked as if he would return the blow, for he drew the crop back; he poised before delivering the slash and suddenly knew in that moment that all his years as a son made him incapable of striking his own father. Instead, still furiously angry, he swung half-right and pitched the crop with a smash clean through a pane of the window.

Ethel Gibbons, who had been listening, white and trembling, outside the door, heard the shattering glass and her heart nearly stopped with fright. Then she heard her son shout: "There! There's your damned crop for you! Don't ever use it on me again!" She threw open the door and found father and son facing each other, both breathing heavily, Robert purple in the face, his eyes staring madly, his features distorted with rage, Tom white-faced and shaken, but still resolute.

"You young swine," said her husband, his voice low and intense; "I'll break every bone in your body for that!"

She sprang forward, seized his arm, and tried to pull him back, crying with fear, "No, Bob, no! Don't hit the boy again! Don't hit him, don't!"

"Let go, woman, let go, and I'll teach the puppy a lesson," growled Robert, but, to tell the truth, he did not try very hard to get free, for he was not so enraged as to have lost all reason. I could go for the boy again, he was thinking, and God knows he deserves it. But he'll fight me tooth and nail this time; even if he isn't as strong as I am, he's nearly as big, and quicker on his feet, and much better winded. Where's my dignity if he blacks both my eyes? What do I say to Mole and Booth and Humphreys when they ask me how it happened?

"Please, please, Bob! I implore you!" said Ethel who, for once, did not read his thoughts accurately. "Tom has been a wicked disobedient boy, and must apologize to you."

But Tom had his father's stubborn streak too. "I will apologize to you, Mother, for the broken window-pane. That is all. Father, you must let me speak, and try to understand. You send me to school to learn to be a gentleman; you say yourself that at my age many lads have a wife and children—yet you still treat me as if I were a little wretch of scarce ten years old. But I'm not! I've been trained at school to use my mind, to reason with it. And since I left school I've had time to think and to see for myself how many evils your free trade produces—witnesses who disappear, juries terrified to return a proper verdict, laborers too lazy to work because they can earn more as tubmen, the King's servants beaten, shot, kidnapped, drowned—and for what? A great flood of cheap brandy and gin which does nothing but ruin men's health and drive them out of their wits. And yet you still smuggle yourself, and try to force me to help you. Well, I *will not*. I will do anything else you ask of me, but not that."

"I see." Robert Gibbons was calmer now, his boiling rage turned to cold bitterness. "In that case my reply is simple." He walked to the door and flung it open. "There is the door. Since you—not your father—are to be judge of what is right and wrong for you I will not ask anything at all of you. You may walk out of that door and go to the devil in whatever way you please. When you've learned your manners you can come back again. You're big enough to earn your own living now, for you needn't look to me for a farthing—now or later. I'll leave the tenancy of this place and all my money to your Uncle Charles and his children. You want your freedom; very well, then—have it! But don't blame me if you're a pauper in the process!"

110

His wife had sunk into a chair, her face in her hands, her tears running through her fingers. There was a silence, in which Tom looked from one parent to the other.

"Aha!" his father smirked in triumph. "That brings you up with a jolt, eh? That makes you think again, does it, sirrah? Come now, don't be such a mule—own that you were in the wrong."

"I was not thinking about myself, Father. I was thinking of Mother, and of how it will be for her when I go."

"Eh? Go? So that's it, is it?" said Gibbons, angry and spluttering again. "Too late to start worrying about your mother now. You should have thought of her before you began all this ridiculous business. There's the door, sir. Go at once. Send word where you are living, and I will send your belongings in a wagon."

The boy bent, and silently kissed the top of his mother's head. Then, eyes to the front and head held up, he walked out of the gun-room, down the hall and out of the front door. At the sound of the outer door slamming, Ethel gave up trying to hold back her sobs and burst out weeping. Gibbons, shaken by the turn things had taken, could only bend and pat her shoulder clumsily. "There, there, don't fret like that over the fellow, Ethel. I'll give the fool three days before his empty belly drives him back. The lesson will do him good."

The woman shook her head, dabbing at her streaming eyes. "How could you, Bob, how *could* you? First Mary, now Tom. Nearly nineteen years now you've lived in a house with that boy—and you don't seem to know anything about him. He'll never knuckle under—never, for he knows he is right and you are wrong. You have lost him for ever, and so have I."

13. WILLIAM BOOTH, the plump and prosperous owner of the biggest and best provision shop in Rye, hastened downstairs and out into his cobbled yard; he lifted the stout beam that held the gates, and pulled them open. The carters cracked their whips and the four great boat-shaped two-horse wagons, each loaded high with tubs, came swinging in out of the dark silent street. He pulled the yard gates shut, but he did not bother to bar them; the wagons would be going out again soon. He hurried across to where the first wagon had stopped alongside the big wooden flaps of his cellar trapdoor. He bent down and unlocked a padlock, and two of the carters raised the flaps. Soon the sloping planks were in position, and tubs were sliding down in rapid succession. Gibbons's foreman, George Humphreys, had come with the wagons, and he now came up, shaking the ball and powder out of his pistol. "Morning, Mr. Booth, sir. Beg yer pardon for rousting you out. Got eight hundred o' gin and three of brandy for you tonight, sir. Got the invoice for you here."

"Very well. By the by—those guards of yours—those cutthroat batmen—I trust you have sent them home? I do not care to have such carrion hanging about my yard."

"Don't you worry, sir. I just sent 'em all home, soon as we came——"

He broke off, and the two men stared at each other, for the street was suddenly full of the clash and clatter of hoofs. Who the devil could it be? Not the dragoons, surely? The horses stopped outside and almost at once the big wooden gates were shouldered open, and half a dozen Customs House men, pistols drawn at the ready, came running across the yard towards them. This was shock enough, but it was the man at the head of the party—the slight pale dark-eyed man in riding-officer's blue—who made Booth and Humphreys and the unloaders stand and goggle, astonished almost to the point of fainting. Lewis! It just could not be him, but it was! Before they could speak or stir, they were surrounded by the menacing guns, helpless prisoners.

If he was excited or triumphant, Lewis did not betray it. His voice was calm and firm. "In the name of King George I declare these goods contraband and forfeit to the Crown. I arrest all here present on the charge of smuggling dutiable goods."

Booth began to splutter incoherently. "An outrage! How dare you treat a man in my position in this way, sir? By God, you'll regret this day's work!"

Lewis smiled thinly. "Possibly, sir. In the meantime, I would ask you to come without causing a disturbance."

"Do you realize, fellow, that I am deputy chairman of the Rye bench of magistrates? A precious fool you will look in court, I warn you."

"Indeed? We shall see, sir."

George Humphreys broke in, disgusted at his fellow prisoner's panic. "Don't you bother yer head, Mr. Booth, sir, Mr. Mole'll soon have you out on bail, and you know well enough you got nothing to fear from yer friends on the Bench."

113

Lewis saw no point in discussing things any further. "Matthews, do you stay and guard the goods; Maxted, come with me; the rest of you, take the carters under guard to the jail-house." He swung round on Booth and Humphreys, who were somewhat surprised by this curious procedure: "Have I your word of honor that you will not attempt to escape? I have leg-irons outside, otherwise."

The two men nodded dumbly. Booth paled at the word "leg-irons" and began to wonder if his acquittal was going to be easy after all. This Welsh fellow seemed pretty confident, like a man with a card up his sleeve. Humphreys, who had been in many a scrape like this in his twenty-five years at the free trade, was still unconcerned. "Very well, then. Be good enough to walk out to the corner of the High Street."

This at last punctured Humphreys' calm. "High Street? What are you talking about? That ain't the way to the jail!"

Lewis shrugged, and motioned with his pistol, and the strange quartet moved out into the street. It was only a few yards to the main street, but in that short space of time the prisoners had many anxious questions in their minds. The answer, when they reached the street, was more chilling and deadly than they could have dreamed. There, drawn up with its blinds down, and four big horses in the traces, was a coach. They knew it at once for Lord Tillingham's, for it had his crest of ships and castles on its door. Booth shivered; the quiet street and the dawn air seemed horribly cold. He suddenly found his clothes sticking with a chill sweat. Even the tough and stolid Humphreys felt a tightening in his belly. Like a nightmare, it all was. Chap who's supposed to be on a French gallows turns up alive and kicking. Seemed to know every move they made, too, else how could he have been at Booth's place just in time? There was a sneaking rat in Camber somewhere. Then this coach—that was the worst part of a bad business. They didn't need a coach to take them a couple of hundred yards to Rye jailhouse. What if . . . ? No—that didn't bear thinking about . . .

Silently they boarded the coach, and as soon as the door clicked the driver shook the reins and they began to rumble steadily up the graying street. As they passed the last houses the driver cracked his whip over his team's backs, and whistled through his teeth. The splendid chestnuts pricked their ears, tossed their heads, and accelerated to a spanking gallop. Inside the bouncing coach there was a gloomy silence, but when, half a mile out of town, the driver hauled around a sharp left turn, Booth could contain his curiosity no longer: "He is taking the Tonbridge road!"

"That is so," said Lewis. "We shall be stopping at Tonbridge."

"And what for, I should like to know?" said Booth, with an attempt at blustering sarcasm.

"Why, to change horses, of course. One can hardly expect one team to go all the way to London."

"London!" The two free traders looked at each other, pale with fear and astonishment.

"London, gentlemen. Bow Street Court, to be precise. You expected to go before a court, and so you shall. But possibly not the court you expected."

The two men looked so gray and wretched in their fear that Lewis felt almost sorry for them. Both knew what it meant—transportation—seven years or more in the savage penal colony in Van Diemen's Land, that wet, remote, forbidding island south of Australia. No man knew what life in this place—which some called Tasmania—was like, for no one had yet served a sentence and come back. But everyone knew about the appalling three-month voyages in the slow, cramped, disease-ridden convict ships.

Both men sat shut in with their misery as the splendid sunlit Weald scenery rolled past. At last, despite his fear, Humphreys' night's work began to tell on him, and he fell asleep. For some time after that Booth shot furtive sidelong glances at him to make sure; then he leaned forward and tapped Lewis on the knee; he was gulping and talking desperately: "Mr. Lewis, sir" (not "fellow" any more, Iorwerth noted) "there are a few things I should like to tell you. In a sense, sir, I am glad this has happened; we honest tradesmen are being terrorized . . . yes, terrorized is the only word for it . . . into dealing with the free traders. I was taking in run goods, I will not attempt to deny it—but much against my will, sir, much against my will. I believe you, sir, have suffered even more at the hands of these ruffians, so that we have a common cause, Mr. Lewis, in a sense. Anything that I can do to help . . . I could give you all the names, and how they work . . . Anything you require . . ."

He looked at the riding-officer, his eyes staring with a desperate hope; but he was appalled to see Lewis returning him a stony inflexible stare. All he said was: "I have all the information I require, Mr. Booth."

In for a penny, in for a pound, thought Booth, and went plunging pitifully on: "I'm not a poor man, Mr. Lewis, nor an ungrateful one when somebody has been a friend to me. You understand me? I have nothing with me now, of course, but get me pen, ink and paper at Tonbridge, and I will give you a note on my bank for as many guineas as you care to name." Then, with a businessman's caution, he added: "Within reason, of course."

This time Lewis made no answer to him, but turned to the Customs man beside him. "You heard that attempt to bribe me, Maxted. I will write the words down when we get

116

to Tonbridge, and you will sign your name as a witness."

"Can't sign, sir. Never could handle these here quills."

"Very well. Make your mark, then, make your mark."

Booth saw at last that he dared say no more.

14. Two days later, Robert Gibbons lifted the latch of his back door, letting in a flood of morning sunlight, and walked out into his yard to give his orders for the day's work. The dairy cows had been milked, and were being turned out into their pasture by little Simon Humphreys; there was still no news of the boy's father. The few shillings the lad could earn, and a few more that his mother made by scrubbing and washing for Ethel, would have to keep the family for a good many years now, like enough.

Abel Marling, promoted foreman since Thursday morning's disaster, came from among a knot of men by the barn to meet him. Gibbons was too preoccupied by his own thoughts to notice his odd nervous manner.

"Weather's breaking up, Abel. Saw a ring around the moon last night. A damned pest, with half the hay yet to make. A good job the shearing is over and done with. We'll cut no more hay today, I think."

"Seven-acre Piece is near ready to carry, farmer."

"Aye, I walked through there myself last night. The dew's going fast, Abel. Put them all to tedding the hay in Seven-acre—the women too, as many as you can get. It should be fit to begin raking and carting by twelve."

"Right you are, master," said Abel, and just stood there, rubbing the back of his neck awkwardly.

"Well, see to it, then, Abel, see to it! I have no time to spare for chat this morning, and neither have you."

"Ah, but, I beg your pardon, sir, I got something I got to say to you." Abel looked this way and that, as if he wished himself many miles away; drawn by his distress, half a dozen of the hands sidled over, and stood behind him in a semi-circle.

"Good God, what's the matter with you, man? I've given my orders for the work, and that is that. Do I have to run my farm with a parliament?"

"'Tis not about the farm work, sir." Abel Marling paused, desperately trying to draw courage from his mates around him. It was hard to stand up and argue with a man who'd been your master for twelve year or more. But there it was, they'd made him spokesman. "'Tis about George Humphreys, master."

"Well, what of him, poor devil?"

"We shan't see him no more, master. 'Least, not for many a year. He won't get a proper trial, not among all them London folk. They don't understand about the free trade up there. If he was going to be up for trial in Rye we wouldn't say nothing. What I mean is, a Rye jury thinks the same about the damned gaugers as what we do."

"Yes, yes, yes! I know all this! Get to the point, Marling!"

"It's like this, y'see: We got to make sure no one else gets sent up to London. Now we all know who done it to George: me lord over at Tillingham Place, there. Lewis couldn't have done it without him. His lordship's got to be warned off, sir."

"Very fine to say all this, Abel. Perhaps you'll tell me how? Lord Tillingham is a powerful man. Not easy to frighten."

"We know a man who could do it, farmer, and so do you."

"You don't mean . . . ?"

"Toby Catt. Him and his Hawkhurst gang."

"Catt!" Gibbons threw his arms up in exasperation. Abel flinched but did not move. Gibbons poked him in the chest with his crop. "You must be a madman to say that name to me! Damme, you were there that night in April when I sent him packing. I wonder that you dare to suggest that I go cap in hand to a man I swore never to employ again!"

There was an angry murmur among the men behind Marling, and it gave him courage. "Now there's no call for you to be angry, master, but it's like this: If you don't send for Toby, none of us'll turn out Wednesday night." He shifted about on his feet uneasily, and stared at the ground. "So there we are, master."

"You're lunatics, all of you! Why, it was Catt who started all this trouble. The man we all know about—the one who passed away suddenly—was a relation of Lord Tillingham's, that's why he's taken a hand. Dammit, he's let us do what we liked for twenty years, even if he is an Admiralty Commissioner! And you all know how much prime cognac and tea has gone over to Tillingham Place. And lace too, in her ladyship's day. Turn Toby Catt loose on him, and you'll bring the whole country down around our ears."

"That's your opinion, master, but we've talked it all over, and we reckon that at this rate we'll all finish up cutting down trees and making roads and dying of plague in Van Diemen's Land—you too, sir. We got to get rid of that gauger too, o' course, but an ounce of lead'll do for him any night when he's on his rounds. What we say is we need Toby and the chaps from Hawkhurst to put the wind up his Lordship."

Robert Gibbons had felt depressed enough before; the house was as dull as a ditch without Tom and Mary. He hadn't realized how much he would miss them. Now he was almost in despair; every instinct told him to keep away from that murderous Toby Catt and the bloody Hawkhurst gang, but if he did, it seemed he was finished as a free trader, and perhaps as a farmer too. And after three generations of running goods! He felt angry with the men for forcing him like this, and yet resigned, like a rider letting go the reins of a headstrong horse. What they wanted was all wrong, but there was nothing he could do.

"I'll see Catt tonight," he said curtly. They all grinned broadly at each other, and he cut their triumph short: "And now for God's sake let us get some work done! I don't pay fellows to stand about prating all day."

The evening sun shone bright and yellow through the leaded windows of Lord Tillingham's study. He was writing at his desk; opposite him, sitting respectfully upright, were two men in uniform. One was Lewis, now looking fit, and with only a trace of bruising on his face to show the battering he'd had a fortnight ago. The other man was of Lewis's age, but unlike him in every other way. For one thing, he was elegantly and splendidly dressed in the uniform of a naval lieutenant, his blue coat bright with gold buttons and epaulettes, his white doeskin breeches so beautifully cut that they fitted like a second skin. A long sword, its hilt gilded and polished, hung from a blue and gold belt, and on the side table lay his cocked hat and white gloves. Yet one look at his bronzed, boyish, yet hard features told Lewis that Lieutenant Finch of the *Harpy* was not one of the wealthy titled boobies so common in the Navy.

The nobleman finally signed his name with a flourish, sanded the paper, folded it and gave it to the lieutenant.

"Very well, then, gentlemen, that is that. I am obliged for your attendance. We are agreed on our plan for Wednesday night? Mr. Lewis to ambush the wagons wherever they are loaded; the Folkestone dragoons to attack the beach party; you, Mr. Finch, to be waiting with *Harpy* in company with the *Fox*. Close in on the lugger as soon as the signal flares are sighted. This paper, lieutenant, gives you my authority for the rather irregular action we have planned, together with a request for the co-operation of the *Fox*. You are sure no one at Folkestone knows you have come here? Good. Be good enough to conceal your uniform with your cloak when you leave, and make sure that the coach blinds are down. Our enemies are numerous and by no means stupid. Now, Mr. Lewis, you will be seeing your informant on Monday night, I believe?" He smiled wryly. "H'm. Since you will be taking him his first prize-money you should get all the information you need. I have no one in my household sufficiently trustworthy to send, so I suggest that you take the information straight over to Folkestone yourself. If you cannot ride your patrol that night, well, it cannot be helped. This is more important than a few ankers of gin."

He rose, and the two young men sprang up. He poured them glasses of Madeira wine himself, for he did not wish to bring his tattling butler into the room. "To Wednesday night," he said, raising his glass.

Soon the lieutenant left, and Lewis excused himself, and went back to the library. What with the patrols and his kidnapping, he had got little enough done there in the four weeks he had been at Tillingham Place. Now that he had an assistant, things would perhaps go better.

His assistant sat in the window, his back to the door, his table littered with calf-bound books. "Well, Tom," said Lewis, "have you found anything of interest in that batch?"

"Not very much," said Tom Gibbons, looking around with a smile. "I think that shelf was the one his Lordship used for books he did not want. There were dozens of old

122

school books—Caesar's *De Bello Gallico* and so forth. As inky and dog-eared and scribbled-upon as mine were. Then there are twelve volumes of *Transactions of the Sussex Archaeological Society*, and this one." He held up a huge well-bound, dusty book which had clearly never been opened. "*Collected Sermons of the Right Reverend Algernon Grimwade, D.D., some time Bishop of Chichester.* And look, on the fly-leaf: 'To my dear nephew William, on the occasion of his twenty-first birthday. May he find wisdom, joy and comfort in these pages.' It doesn't look as if he did find them, does it?"

"He found them elsewhere, Tom, no doubt. There is nothing of value, then?"

"Only one book—Volume One of a seventeenth-century edition of Ovid's *Metamorphoses.* Perhaps we shall find Volume Two later."

"What? Oh yes. Well, put it by, Tom, for the present."

"You are not really listening to me, are you? I suppose you have something on your mind . . . something to do with my——"

"Now, Tom," said Lewis gently. "You remember what we agreed, that evening when you arrived here in search of a roof and a bed: that I should ask nothing of you, and you nothing of me? God forbid that we should use a son to catch his own father. Besides, if I had plans in my mind I am under oath not to reveal them to anyone."

"Aye, I know, but it is hard not to . . ."

"Tom, you have settled in well, and been most helpful to Mr. Kedge the steward and to me. You have a choice of six fine horses if you wish to ride in the park, and guns to go shooting. Be content, Tom, and let us put the free trade out of our minds. One day it may not be there to come between us; one day soon, perhaps."

123

15. The storm which Robert Gibbons had foretold came up slowly from across the Channel. Even by noon the next day no rain had fallen, though now the sky was a dull low vault of hurrying cloud. The wind had risen and backed. On the flat sand at Dymchurch the angry gray seas broke in acres of yeasty foam; on the shingle beach at Camber the steep solid waves hammered and sucked at the rattling pebbles. The wind swept across the featureless marsh, flailing and threshing the willows along all the dykes until their leaves shone white in the gloom; and two miles away it roared gustily in the huge beeches and elms around Tillingham Place.

Mr. Capper went around the great house that afternoon, carefully securing all windows against the brutal gusts, and by the time he finished at six, the first drops were beginning to slash diagonally across the windows of the south side.

Tom felt miserable when he went to bed in his room at the back of the house. He had been inactive all day, and he lay open-eyed and wakeful for hours. If only one could see the future, see how it would turn out; things were in such a confounded tangle now between himself, Mary, Father,

124

Mother. When would they all be friends—a family—again? What could he have done to make things better?

The hours dragged on drearily; he found himself listening to the chimes of the grandfather clock on the landing, counting the quarters as they came relentlessly around— half past twelve, a quarter to one, one o'clock . . . The rain lashing the windows, shaking the sashes in their frames, the wind blowing dismal bass notes on the chimneys. A quarter past one. Would he never get to sleep?

And then, as he lay looking up at the ceiling, half-drowsy at last, he was aware of a curious thing: The white plaster was being lit up by a faint, flickering red glow—a glow which was becoming stronger every moment. He sat up with a jerk, jumped out of bed and went to the window. There was the cause of the flickering glow: Out there, on the north side of the park, something was burning fiercely in spite of the rain; the light of the flames was thrown back by the low clouds, forming a low red arc in the northern sky.

A few moments later he was pounding at Lord Tillingham's door. "My lord, my lord, the stacks are afire!" For he knew that over there, in a corner of a big pasture sheltered by a wood, was a cluster of haystacks which between them held most of the newly-made hay of the Home Farm.

Before long the whole house was awake. Menservants ran about finding themselves coats and oilskins. Others ran to the estate cottages to roust out the farm workers. The gamekeeper and his two underkeepers, on Lord Tillingham's instructions, were loading shotguns. "Any man you find near the stacks," the master had said, "must be challenged and brought to the house. Shoot at any man who does not reply, or seeks to escape. Shoot to kill any man who fires on you first."

Tom did not ask if he might go, for he was sure he would be refused. Instead, he donned oilskins and mingled with

125

the party of footmen, gardeners and grooms who were to try to save what hay they could. They streamed, a long straggling column, down the main drive, up a farm track to their right, and through a gateway to where, a week ago, they had built a little town of haystacks, six big ones in two rows of three. All of them remembered how well they'd looked, the hay a bright dusty-greeny-gold against the black-green of the woods, and how they'd smelled, the tons of curing hay sending up a sweetness so heavy that it almost made you drunk.

As they struck out across the field to the far corner, Pattenden, the Home Farm bailiff, felt his spirits rising. There were no flames to be seen now. Couldn't be too bad, or it would still be burning; the free traders didn't know their job if they tried to fire a stack a night like this. Then he stopped, sniffing, and they all smelled the horrible reek of a grass fire smouldering in the rain. And wait! There was something else mingled in that stale burning stink. Pattenden sniffed like a pointer, puzzled.

"Smells like some sort o' spirit to me, gaffer," said one of the laborers.

"I know," said a footman. "That's lamp-oil, that is!"

"Ah!" said the bailiff, "that's how they got it to start, then."

The reek became stronger as they neared the stacks. There was still some smoke in the wind, which made their eyes run and smart. "Get all the lanterns around here," said Pattenden, "and let's see what they have managed to do. Can't be much, hardly."

The men with lanterns gathered around the nearest stack and held them as high as they could. What he saw by their light made Pattenden draw in his breath sharply in dismay: The stack itself wasn't much damaged at first sight, but when you looked closer you could see that men who knew what they were doing had set out to do as much malicious

126

and wanton damage as they could in a short time. Instead of a smooth, trim slope of straw thatch, the top of the stack was now simply an ugly misshapen hump of burnt hay. Some clever and wicked devils of men had got up on the stack and soused the whole thatch with lamp oil. That had been enough, even in this rain, to burn off all the protecting straw, and to make the flickering red patterns on Tom's ceiling. And now, if course, all this heavy rain was driving straight on to the unprotected hay, ruining it. Still, this was only one stack—there were five others. Perhaps the rest would be . . .

Hunched in the lashing rain and cold wind, the bailiff and his men went round the whole street of stacks, solemnly holding up their lanterns to each one in turn. As they went, the feeling of sick despair grew and grew in James Pattenden; for every stack was in the same state as the first. He felt the pricking of tears when he thought of the work and planning and worry that had gone into their making. Of course, they would cover the remaining hay as quickly as they could, but had they enough cloths? Where were all the cloths now? How long was it going to take to get them all here and spread? Two at least had been lent out, and were five miles off.

With all these practical problems whirling in his head, he began giving his orders for the fetching of sail-cloths, and was busy talking with his men when he heard the jingle of harness and the thud of hoofs. Out of the dark into the sketchy glow of the lanterns came the Earl himself, with his steward Mr. Kedge riding at his elbow.

"Well, Pattenden," he said, "what is the damage? Surely in this rain——"

"Never mind the rain, me lord," said Pattenden, too upset for proper respect. "That won't help. The damned swine have burnt off every last straw of thatch with oil."

"But most of the hay itself is unburnt?"

"Unburnt? Aye, for what use that is. Don't ye see it's getting soaked every minute we stand here prating? How long is it going to take me to cloth it all up? And what about all the oil and ash and muck that's soaking into it? How're your fancy horses and cattle going to like that this winter? What the devil's the use of saying it's unburnt?"

"Pattenden!" said the steward sternly. "Remember whom you are addressing! How dare you speak to his lordship in such a way?"

"Do not disturb yourself, Mr. Kedge. I understand well enough how the bailiff feels, and I see how foolish my question was. We will leave you to save what you can, Pattenden." He wheeled his horse away, and Kedge followed closely. "There is one very strange thing about this, none the less," he went on to the steward, "and that is the choice of a night of howling gale and pouring rain for firing stacks. After the events of last week I have been expecting such gestures of hate. But why be content to damage stacks when by choosing any dry windy night they could burn them to the ground without even using oil?"

Kedge shook his head. "The damage is almost as serious as a total loss, my lord. We shall save little enough good sweet fodder out of those ruined stacks."

Lord Tillingham shrugged. "Well, hay is hay, Kedge, and can be bought cheap enough in any market. They can burn all the hay in Kent and Sussex for all I care."

Tom Gibbons, working with the laborers, felt a deep and bitter shame at the wickedness of the waste. His own father! He was glad it was too dark for the men to recognize him. Just before dawn, after a night of hasty and back-breaking work, he walked back to the house. He had been out in the rain so long, and was so wet, that he hardly noticed that the rain had now stopped, the wind had veered, and stars were showing through ragged gaps in the clouds. Soon the sun would be shining.

He went round to the washhouse at the back and shed his wet and filthy outer clothes. He washed thoroughly under the pump there before going up to his room in shirt and drawers. By the time he went upstairs the sun was up. He paused on the stairs and looked out. The air, the trees, the fields, everything, seemed washed and renewed by the rain after the long hot drought. The birds, cheered at last by the warmth, were singing in the elms of the park; the grass and trees dropped gently away to the south, merging first into pasture and then into marsh. Tom looked at all this inattentively, thinking how much like fantastic nightmare last night's business seemed in the warmth and stir of day. Then his wandering eye was caught by something odd, and he looked quickly back. Queer! Why should there be that cloud of birds wheeling and circling over the marsh, a mile away there? What birds? They were too dark for gulls, and no one would be ploughing now——

And then, suddenly, with a kind of freezing horror, he knew for certain what birds they were, and why they were there. He scrambled into his other coat and trousers and ran to hammer on Lewis's door. After a night's patrol Lewis was irritable at being roused, and Lord Tillingham was even more so; but both men were so appalled at what he told them that they were soon dressed and running down the south lawn between the elegantly landscaped trees. At the bottom of the lawn they scrambled over a rail fence into an empty pasture and came at the other side to a place where the fence dividing pasture from marsh had been flattened and trampled for twenty yards. And then, at last, they came out on to the open marsh, in the middle of which the deep muddy little River Tillingham wound along. There at last they found what they sought, found what they dreaded to find. The birds, they saw, were crows and ravens, buzzards and kites, which croaked, cawed and screamed as they flapped and drifted in an obscene whirl over a loop of the river. And on the trampled and bloody grass within the river-bend, heaped, hacked and slaughtered, lay the entire Tillingham herd of Sussex cattle.

The three men ran across the marsh, slowing to a walk as they approached the first carcass; a gorged raven flapped away as they came near. Lewis and Tom paused, looking at Lord Tillingham, to see how he would take it. His face was white and gaunt and suddenly old. He knelt by the first body, and stroked the dead animal's ears. "Old Tup! I knew it would be you in the vanguard. Look, Iorwerth, they had to shoot him before they dared butcher his wives and children. And look here!" He pulled a bloodstained rag of cloth from one of the bull's horns. "He left his mark on one of them. But there were too many, and you cannot fight guns with naught but bone and sinew and horn and courage." He rose and walked round the shambles, the other two following. But there was not so much as a twitch of life; every cow and calf had been crudely butchered as it stood, penned helpless in the bend of the river. One cow which had jumped or fallen on to the mud of the tidal creek had been followed and killed; silently the incoming tide was covering its bloody, mud-stained head.

The nobleman said not a word as he walked around, but at last he stood surveying the appalling scene. The sun, which now glinted richly on the smooth red hides, had brought out thousands of flies, which added their rasping buzz to the ugly clamor of the carrion birds. Lord Tillingham appeared calm, his face impassive. "What fools we were, Iorwerth, to laugh off the stack-burning so easily! It is obvious now that that was a mere decoy to attract attention to the north side of the estate while this went on. In fact, the night was perfect for them: Had it been calm we should have heard the cattle bellowing from the house. The poor beasts must have been crazy with fear."

"It is a sad blow to your lordship, I know," said Lewis gently.

"Twenty years, Iorwerth, of love and work and care, day and night. I have been a lonely man since my wife died; these, and their mothers and fathers before them, have made me less lonely. Indeed, I cannot tell Jem the cowman this news myself. His look would make me weep like a green girl. I am ashamed to own it, but I mourn them—especially Old Tup—more than I did my nephew, whom I hardly knew. And yet, Iorwerth, these free traders have made a grave mistake: They wanted to hurt me to frighten me off; but they have hurt me so much at the first blow that I hardly care what they do next. I only know that now it is war to the death. I will see every man of them hanged or transported, or perish in the attempt. I am sorry to say it in front of this young man here, but I do not choose to share the same county as the men who could do this." He stared at the poor broken bodies, then recovered himself with an effort, and spoke briskly. "This morning, Iorwerth, we will ride over to see the Colonel of Dragoons at Hythe."

16.

ROBERT GIBBONS sat on the beach and gnawed his fingernails until he nearly drew blood. Dammit, he was thinking, we've done everything we can do to make the run a success, and yet . . . and yet I feel more nervous than I have done for twenty-five years—since I was Tom's age. We've got a different beach, three miles off from Camber, different loading point, different destination for the wagons, twice as many tubmen and batmen as usual. And still I've this feeling of something hanging over my head—like the dream last night where the barn wall was falling and crushing me. Lewis and Lord Tillingham—what will they do? That's the point. An ugly and dirty business, to slaughter a herd twenty years in the making. Thank God I wasn't there when they did it. But cows are cows, and free men are free men; a parcel of gaugers can't be allowed to tell Sussex lads where and when they can buy and sell.

The hush among the clustered men on the beach was broken as a new arrival, who clearly cared nothing about keeping quiet, came scrunching down the pebbles, whistling tunelessly. He seemed cheerful, confident, pleased with himself, and, as usual when there was a run, fairly drunk. He came the last few yards with a rush, blundering into Gibbons, who fended him off irritably: "Hey-up, there, farmer!" said Catt, his voice blurred and thick. "Jacob not here yet, then? Never mind, I got summat to tell you. Bit o' news. Good news, too. I found your rat for you."

"My rat?"

"The fellow who's been giving away all your secrets, and getting well paid for it."

"Who is it? I'll soon see——"

"Not who *is* it, farmer—who *was* it. Well, now: You know your man Abel Marling?"

"Not him—it couldn't be him!"

"D'you know his wife's dad—chap called Hewett?"

"Old Seth Hewett—yes. He's the verger over at Camber. You mean he's the one . . . ?"

Catt nodded and came closer, stabbing at Gibbons with his finger: "He's been sitting in his chimney corner listening to all Marling's chat, and then running off to sell it to the gaugers."

"How did you find out all this?"

"From the damned old croaker himself. Tell you how it was: last night Harry Stoddard and I called in latish at The Cock at Wittersham—just on business, y'see, about some gin they'd ordered. Well, there was a proper bedlam going on in the tap-room—every man there singing and yelling and full of gin and brandy. And there, in the middle of it all, was this half-starved-looking old bag of bones pulling out guineas from his purse as fast as the landlord called for 'em, and shouting that there was plenty more where they came from. Says to meself, I says: 'Toby, you want to look into this, you do.' So I talked a bit with some of the chaps about him, and found he came from Camber. 'Aha,' I says, 'Bob Gibbons'll want to know about this.' So we joined in the sport there for an hour or so, and when it came time to go home we told the old chap we had a trap outside and we

133

was going to Rye, and he could ride with us if he wanted to. Soon as we got outside, of course, we told him who we were and what we thought of gaugers and them who helped 'em. That got most of the good cheer out of him, and he sobered up sudden-like. Shook like a leaf, he did, and cried like a babby. 'Right, then,' I says to him, 'fair is fair. You tell me all you've done to get that money, and I promise we won't touch a hair of your head.' So then we got the whole yarn off of him—how he met this chap Lewis in the church of a night time, and how he left a signal for him and how Lewis give him half his prize-money. All the stuff you lost was through him, you see."

Gibbons was enraged. "Good God—the cowardly, sneaking, treacherous old crow! Well, you may have promised not to hurt him, but I'm damned if I'll let it pass like that. I'll soon——"

Catt cackled loudly. "Half a minute, farmer, I ain't finished the story yet. After all this, y'see, a very funny thing happened at Iden Bridge. Somehow, the old chap chanced to bang his head very hard against my swingler, and then he somehow flew over the parapet into the river, and there he is still, I daresay, unless he went out with the ebb this morning. Sad, ain't it?"

Gibbons was silent. Catt and his ways again! Everyone knew informers had got to go, but still there was something horrible about his methods and the pleasure he got out of them.

"So there's another few guineas you owe me, farmer. Or at least"—he took out a big heavy old purse and threw it up in the air—"you would if the old chap hadn't very kindly given me this before he jumped in the Rother!"

Gibbons looked away in irritation and distaste. "It's likely, then, that Lewis knows about this run?"

"He does. Old Hewett told me. But there—damn the fellow's eyes—what can he do about it? He'll get no help from Winchelsea, I'll guarantee that; the Customs men care only about their hides, and you've kept all the dragoons in gin for years. And Lewis ain't going to be amongst us much longer, I promise you."

"Master!" A low voice from the sea wall. "The lugger's there—showing her light."

"Very well then, boy. Give them a flink to show we're ready and the coast's clear." Gibbons went down to the sea partly relieved. This would be the last run that Lewis would be told about, and soon he would be gone anyway. Perhaps then they could go back to the good old peaceful days of live-and-let-live. Soon the skiff arrived and Jacob with it. The tub-line was hove in and everyone joined in the work with a will, Jacob and Gibbons taking off the tubs, the tubmen setting off at a fast walk over the sea wall and across a flat, desolate waste of shingle to the Lydd road, where, in the yard of a little farm called Pigwell, a dozen big wagons were waiting, guarded by an extra body of batmen. The flats of shingle made weary walking for loaded men in ordinary boots, so all the tubmen did as the local marsh-dwellers did—fastened small boards of wood to their boots.

Higgins and Gibbons talked as they swung the tubs up on to the waiting backs. "So things are looking better then, farmer?"

"I hope so, Jacob, now that this creeping spy has been nailed."

"I'm glad to hear of his passing. To tell you the truth, I had been thinking of finding myself another freighter to work for, down the Channel a bit. They were finding out too much about you. Well, all's well that ends well. I hear, by the by, that his lordship is well provided with beef these days?"

Gibbons felt so much better that he could joke about

even that now. "Aye, they tell me he's salting it all down and selling it to the Navy. There's enough for every ship in the fleet to have a barrel or two!"

By three in the morning, when the smuggler's hold was almost empty, the free traders both aboard and ashore were too busy and too tired to notice a bright red flash from a little to the west and about a mile out to sea. But someone on shore did see it, and at once, without any sound, there were two great gushes of red flame on the sea wall, one a quarter of a mile to the east of the place of the run, the other the same distance to the west. They all saw those well enough, and immediately every man stopped work and stared, amazed and frightened, stared first at one fire, then at the other, then out to sea. What the devil did this mean? This was something new to all of them.

It was the men left to hoist up the tubs aboard the *Two Brothers* who were to learn the meaning first. For, while they stood irresolute, white-faced, the blackness of the sea to the west of them was suddenly split by vivid yellow flashes, and they heard the ear-splitting roar of a broadside of a cannon. Flat on their faces on deck, they heard the balls go whistling through their masts and rigging, and then another savage eruption of sound and flame from the eastward, and more shot flew viciously over them. One ball hit the foremast ten feet above the deck and snapped the pitch-pine spar like a carrot, bringing it and the main topmast down in a rumbling avalanche of wood and cordage. A hail came from close by to the westward of them, a cultured voice speaking carefully through a speaking-trumpet: "*Two Brothers* ahoy! This is His Majesty's Revenue cutter *Harpy*. I have the cutter *Fox* in company to the eastward of you. I call upon you to surrender, and lay down all arms. You have not the slightest chance of resisting or escaping. I am sending a boarding-party; if they meet any resistance they will with-

136

draw, and I will blow you to pieces without any further parley. The first broadsides were aimed high; the next will not be. What do you say? I give you one minute exactly in which to reply."

The lugger's crew stood up and talked urgently in the waist, but there was little enough to debate about. They were as fierce, skillful and daring as any seamen in England, but they were not madmen. They were seamen enough, in fact, to see that they were caught in a steel trap—the skipper and some of the hands ashore, the anchor down, sails lowered, half the masts gone, the cannon unloaded. The cutters could be made out now, each one a dim double spire of swaying white, each one a mere cable's-length away. It wouldn't be a fight, just a slaughter. They pushed Trotter to the side to answer for them. He cupped his hands. "We surrender, Cap'n. Send your boat."

When Jacob Higgins heard the crash of the first broadside, he began to act like a madman, cursing, shouting orders, hitting out at anyone in his way, sobbing all the time in his demented rage. His boat was to him what the Sussex herd had been to Lord Tillingham. "Great God, it's the cutters—they're firing on my boat. It's that damned swine Finch—I'll kill him myself, see if I don't. He's got no right . . . it's not legal . . . firing without a proper challenge. Not fair . . . not fair to fight a boat at anchor."

"There's naught you can do, Jacob," said Gibbons. "Think yourself lucky to be ashore out of trouble."

"Ashore? Ashore? Aye, that's the thing!" A new idea had seized him: "Where's my lads? You four, here! Leave the damned ankers alone; get me out to the *Brothers* as fast as you can. Come on! Launch her, you swag-bellied scum, get me aboard!"

The four men of the lugger's crew saw well enough the state of madness he was in, and they knew they were court-

137

ing the rope or the press-gang if they went aboard. They looked shiftily at each other and shook their heads. "No, master," said one, nervously. "We've served you well enough for years, and never said you nay, but there ain't——"

At that moment they all saw the bolting madness of his staring eyes, saw his hands reaching for the pistols in his belt. Without another word they swung around and tore off across the shingle into the darkness, the group opening up like a fan as they fled. Bang! Bang! Two balls whistled after them; there was one yell, but all the feet went on spurring through the pebbles.

Even this mutiny did not stop Jacob Higgins. He was a man of iron strength; in a minute he had the skiff afloat and, standing in the bows, was hauling himself rapidly hand-over-hand along the empty end of the tub-line, heaving and grabbing desperately until he was gasping for breath. He had expected the cannonade to continue, and was puzzled when the guns were silent. He could hear the hail from the *Harpy* but the words were faint and garbled. Nat Trotter's reply, coming from nearer at hand, was a little plainer, but even so he caught only the syllables ". . . ender . . . boat . . ." and it took him a little while to guess what the message was. The thought of it—of the *Two Brothers* giving in tamely, to be towed off to some dockyard and sawn in half, drove him to an even greater madness.

Yelling like a maniac, he dragged himself the last few yards, jumped for the main rigging, and hauled himself over the gunwale of his ship. He leaned there for a moment, panting, sobbing for breath, appalled at the scene before him. There, up in the bows, standing weaponless and tame as ewes, were his crew—every man jack apart from the few ashore. Standing guard over them were four marines, their muskets fitted with gleaming bayonets; there were two seamen with pistols at the ready, and with them a sturdy petty officer holding a lantern. Standing by the petty officer, a pistol in his hand, was Lieutenant Finch, speaking to the prisoners in a cool stern voice. The naval party was facing away from him, and did not seem to have heard him.

Higgins reached down to his waistband, and remembered then that he had flung his empty pistols down on Lydd beach. His eye caught a pile of cutlasses taken from his men and thrown down in the scuppers near him. He snatched one up. His voice came out in a choking scream: *"Finch!"* The officer, startled, turned and fired in the same movement, for there was no arguing with that voice. His pistol was a powerful one; the ball caught Higgins high in the chest, and its force toppled him back over the low bulwark. Finch ran to the spot, and his coxswain held the lantern over the side, but there was nothing there but the gently lapping lamplit water. Finch ran the little ramrod through the pistol-barrel to clean it, and measured out a new charge of powder, speaking to himself as much as to the coxswain: "So. I have saved the judge and the hangman a little of their trouble."

Two miles away across the shingle desert Iorwerth Lewis lay prone against the hedge-bank overlooking the little stackyard of Pigwell Farm. His inside was twisted up in one knot of tension; he licked his lips, which, like his tongue, were dry and sticky. But there was comfort in the feel of his two pistols, and in the sight, if he turned his head slightly one way or the other, of his half-dozen men on either side of him. He felt stiff and cramped; after these hours of lying still he could feel the size and shape of every stone and tussock of grass beneath his body.

The hours went by; the tubmen coming and going rapidly

with their loads, which they flung on to the wagons before trotting off again to the beach. The dozen or so batmen stood about, guns at the ready at first, but as the hours dragged by, and nothing happened, they began to relax, swigging at a bottle which they passed from hand to hand. By the time the wagons were nearly full, they were sitting on the ground, sprawled back against the wagon-wheels. Lewis dared not try to look at his watch, but had to lie and worry. Surely he should have heard something by now? What if all the plans had come to nothing? He could take the wagons, but—ah! There it was—the distant rumble of a broadside, followed almost at once by another. The signal to move, for no more tubs would come, and the wagons would soon move off to safety.

"Now, lads!" he whispered, and all of them scrambled to their feet, and over the bank. At the sound of the gunfire, the batmen had jumped up and begun to mill about, arguing and shouting. But if they were startled by the cannon, they were frozen and thunderstruck by the crisp voice from the hedge, right on top of them: "Every man here stand still and lay down his weapons. In the name of His——" There was a tremendous bang right alongside his left ear; one of his men had seen a batman reaching out for his musket. The ball missed and smacked into the side of a wagon, but it was enough to discourage the man and all his comrades from moving for the moment. Still, Lewis thought, it showed their danger, outnumbered two to one in the dark by fierce and hardened men. Perhaps bluff would help. He raised his voice and called out to an entirely mythical person over the other hedge-bank: "Sergeant, order your platoon to shoot down the next man to move!"

It worked! He saw the way their faces fell as they looked at each other. They were still utterly bewildered at what had happened, and he gave them no time to recover. "In the name of His Majesty King George I declare these goods forfeit to the Crown, and every man here under arrest."

His men knew what to do, and they worked fast; he knew that in a few minutes the ridiculous threat of the phantom dragoons would be recognized as a bluff, and then there would be a bloody battle. So, while he and four of the excisemen stood by with their pistols, the other two men took out ready-made lengths of thin twine, went to each batman in turn, and, using a method Lewis had shown them, tied his thumbs together behind his back. No one would struggle with that bond for long, for the thin tight twine cut to the bone if you pulled at it. Lewis gave silent thanks to a schoolboy friend who had taught him that trick years ago.

When dawn broke, a strange cortège went winding through New Romney. Early-rising townsfolk, so used to seeing and hearing the free traders go through with their run goods, rubbed their bleary eyes incredulously, and looked again. Twelve great wagons piled high with ankers of gin, and pulled by four-horse teams—nothing unusual there. But this time, the Welsh gauger was riding ahead of the first wagon, and six Customs House men on the flank and rear; and—most fantastic of all—walking at the tail of each wagon, each one with his hands tied and the wagon-rope in a loop round his neck, were twelve sullen downcast men dressed in black, their faces colored black. The batmen! They'd been men that folk had never seen, but had spoken of in fearful whispers for generations. Now, tied, and in the light of day, you could see they were just ordinary men—rather absurd-looking fellows, in fact.

Robert Gibbons's tubmen, standing there in a line waiting for their loads, looked on open-mouthed at the weird scene between Higgins and his men. Gibbons could see it was doing them no good; the flares and the gunfire had sown the

141

seed of panic in them; this was causing it to grow giant-
like in their minds. In a moment they would run like rabbits,
and if they did that, who knew whether they would ever
turn out again? That meant he had to do something quickly.
"Right, lads," he said briskly, "keep going; one more pair
each and we'll be away. What's happening out there is Jacob
Higgins's lookout. We're all right. There's plenty more luggers in the Channel."

One of the men hauling in the line gave a shout: "Ey,
master, the line won't budge. They must 'a' made it fast."

"Use your head then, man! Wade out as far as you can
and cut it. Then we'll call it a day."

He could sense the relief in the men at the tail of the queue:
this meant they'd be able to go straight home. Then they
all stood still again: from out of the dark to the east came
the high whinny of a horse. What the devil . . . ? They
had not brought a single beast with them! They listened,
every man feeling his heart pump, his scalp prickle. The low
sound of voices, the scrunch of many feet treading the shingle. The batmen were out there to deal with interferers,
true; but this sounded like a lot of men!

The silence was suddenly slashed to ribbons by the sound
of a musket shot, followed by a crackling spurt of other
shots; almost at once they heard the clashing of the pebbles
under a dozen running feet, and Catt and his followers came
dashing towards them. One man's arm hung useless at his
side, and Catt's own face was streaming with blood from a
scalp wound. His features were a mask of red, white
and smudged black, and it was the horror of his look, as
much as his words, that sent them pelting off into the darkness: "The soldiers! Hundreds of 'em!"

At first light of dawn Gibbons and Catt, their chests heaving from the running they'd done, their clothes soaked to

142

the waist in water and black mud from wading a dyke, came into the kitchen at Peasmarsh Farm and fell into chairs. For a while they sat there, panting and brooding. Then Gibbons rose and poured out tots of brandy. Catt took his glass without a word, swallowed the liquor, and held the glass out again. "A pretty night's work, farmer! Boat gone, tubmen scared out of their wits, all the goods gone. We risk our necks and catch the ague getting across to Pigwell, and we find the Welsh swine gone off to Hythe with every drop of it— and twelve good men into the bargain."

"Only one thing for it, Toby, though I never thought to live to say it: Have to lie low for a few months. My dad had to, once, in '74."

The Hawkhurst man spat on the clean flagstones: "Lie low be damned, farmer. That ain't our way. We'll beat them man to man. I'll get hold of every good stout chap from Poole to Dover. There's all the goods from the last run, and the Lord knows what else beside, in that Customs House in Hythe, but by God they're not staying there. We'll get those tubs again, farmer, if I have to fight King George hisself."

17. Tom was in the library that afternoon, finding it hard to keep his mind on books and manuscripts, when the door opened and Capper came in to announce, in a tone of infinite disgust: "Mr. Gibbons, a *person* is at the door wishing to see you. Kindly ask her to use the servants' entrance in future."

When Tom got to the front door and looked down the steps he was astonished to see, perched on the side of a little donkey-cart, the shapeless bundled figure of Mother Fagg. If the old woman was out of place she did not seem to feel it, for she said in her usual sharp, indomitable voice, "'Ere y'are, young feller, message from yer poor mum. Fine state she's in! You Gibbonses!" She produced a folded note from inside her filthy old wrappings, shook the reins, and drove off without another word. Tom's hands were clumsy with haste. "Dear Tom," the note read, "Meet me tonight at ten in our small wagon-shed. He will be out. I *beg* you to come. Your loving and distraught Mother."

It was a plea he could not refuse, and he knew she would not invite him into danger, but his feelings as he opened the yard-gate that night were of reluctance and dread. The place had been home to him all his life, but now he felt a foreign spy there, felt that any moment he might be challenged and shot.

He heard the stir and rustle of silk as soon as he entered the wagon-shed. She came rapidly out of the shadows and hugged him tightly, sobbing, "Tom! I thought I should never see you again! But yet I knew you'd come. He says terrible things about you, but I knew you wouldn't fail me. I've been so afraid you two might meet——"

"Then why did you——?"

"Never fear, Tom. He won't be here tonight. He and that villain Catt went off this morning, and won't be back till Saturday. Oh, Tom, he's in that horrible man's power now, and it will be the death of him if you don't help. You must, Tom!"

"Of course I will, Mother. But how? What can I do?"

"Listen, Tom: You know what happened on Wednesday night; well, when he and Catt came back next morning they were both in a tearing fury. They got so drunk and talked so loud that I could hear every word they said. Tom, this man Catt has talked him into sheer madness: they have gone west to collect an army of what Catt calls 'stout chaps,' and next Sunday they are going to ride openly into Hythe, break open the Customs House, and take away the tubs that were captured."

Tom whistled in astonishment. "In broad daylight? But with that sort of army it will not be easy to stop them. There are only two or three men on guard there on a Sunday. But I still do not see——"

His mother turned away, as if half-ashamed of what she was going to ask. Yet her voice was as firm as she could make it. "I want you, Tom, to tell Mr. Lewis what I have told you. Every detail."

"Inform? Betray Dad? Never! I couldn't do it."

"But you must!"

145

"Besides, if I did, Mr. Lewis would not listen. He has said that he will never use me against the free traders."

"He will when he hears what is planned. This is not running a few tubs ashore at midnight, it is an open attack on him. He will have to act on it."

"Perhaps so. But nevertheless I cannot do it."

His mother caught him by the shoulders and shook him as if he were still a little boy. "Tom, you don't know what he is like! He is out of his senses. He will not listen to me any more. He is just monkey-led by that vile creature Catt. You know as well as I do that one day Catt's body will hang in chains. If you don't take a hand your own father will be beside him. God knows, it may be too late already! Do you suppose, Tom, that I like betraying him? I loathe and detest myself for doing it, but I know that I must. I know I am sentencing him to Van Diemen's Land, but even that is better than the gallows. I have had a pitiful time of it with him these last months, through this cursed trade, but he is the man I loved and married, the father of my children. I cannot let him . . ." She broke down and could say no more, but wept bitterly on Tom's shoulder, shaking him with her sobs.

Colonel Westbroke, officer in charge of the 43rd Heavy Dragoons stationed at Hythe, felt bewildered and irritated. He was a soldier of the old school—tough, reliable, and brave. But he was one of the very few men of his position who had risen from the ranks; his first taste of battle had come to him forty years ago. War, plain simple ordinary everyday war —battles and sieges and camps and retreats—that he understood well enough. But this skirmishing about on marshes with a lot of native English cut-throats, this was not his trade. This job at Hythe was supposed to be a kind of retirement, and here he was, hauled out of his bed at dawn

146

to argue with this odd pair with their quicksilver minds that he couldn't follow—this acid-faced Admiralty lord and his henchman the gauger. What the devil did it matter anyway if people could buy good brandy a bit cheaper?

Lord Tillingham cleared his throat emphatically and broke in upon his sullen daydream: "Allow me, then, Colonel, to sum up what we have decided. Please correct me if I omit anything. First, that since these ruffians are asking for open war, they shall have it—perhaps more than they want. Second, that they must be fought in the open field before they have the chance to get to Hythe; otherwise there are bound to be foolish onlookers, some of whom may be hurt or killed. Third, that we shall require a force of at least a hundred men——"

"But as I said," put in Westbroke, "I haven't that many. There is, after all, a war going on against the French, my lord. I shall have to send to Folkestone and Dover and Lewes for them——"

"My dear sir, send to Aberdeen for them if you wish, but get them! If these men are allowed to have their way, it is an end to all pretense of law and order here. Surely you see that? Because they do not wear uniform you seem to think that the parish beadle could turn them back. I tell you once again, Colonel, that you will have to fight some of the most reckless, bold, and dangerous men in England. As to the problem of obtaining men: I am not officially in charge, but I hope I have some power and authority in Kent and Sussex. You may use my name as your warrant. Fourth, there must be absolute secrecy and absolute discipline. We must do much better, Colonel, than your men did at Lydd the other night. They did not succeed in catching one man, you will remember. Now then"—he pointed with a quill to a point on the map on his desk—"we are to trap them just here on the Lydd road at the place called the Forelands

Half the dragoons to leave Lydd and ride southwest at full gallop at half-past five, the other half to move into Coldharbor Farm, a mile and a half east of Peasmarsh Farm at midnight on Saturday. Every man, woman and child at Coldharbor to be kept under observation. Absolute silence; no fires, no bugles. Troops to be ready to move off at five, but to wait until the smugglers pass before revealing themselves. Then they follow them along the road towards Lydd. Look, Colonel, the place we have picked is a perfect trap: on either side of the road, a dozen or so yards away across the marsh, is a deep dyke. Dragoons in front, dragoons behind, water on each side. Perfect. Not one must escape, Colonel, not one."

Sunday morning. The first streaks graying the black eastern sky. At Peasmarsh Farm the house, the barn, the stables, the yard full of the creak and jingle of harness, the stir and bustle of men, the footfalls of men and horses, the clash of weapons. The free traders were mustering in the chill air; every man's voice was hushed; all were tasting the excitement of the coming triumph.

For Ethel Gibbons it was the climax of a mounting nightmare: all day yesterday the men had been arriving in two's and three's from the west—men with bronzed faces, huge wild beards, men with strange broad accents, thin, rat-faced townsmen with dead-white skins, Guernsey men speaking a French patois, a tall Negro with great staring eyes. And all of them with shotguns and muskets, many carrying old rusty swords in cracked leather scabbards. All of them fierce, wild, reckless and drunk. The maids had been too terrified to go amongst them with their food, but for Ethel there was no fear to compare with her fear for what the morning would bring. She moved about pale, gaunt, aloof, and she said nothing when, just after half past five, her husband swung himself into the saddle, grinned at Toby Catt, and cried,

"Here we go, then, boys! A long life to every good free trader, and death to the damned gaugers!"

Hiding in the reeds a little way back towards Camber, Tom saw the figures, dark against the soft growing light, as the cavalcade, shouting and singing, came out of Peasmarsh Farm gate and turned left for Lydd, Romney and Hythe. He had promised Lewis and his lordship that he would keep right out of the fighting, and he would not go back on his word. He could not bear to stay at Tillingham Place, four miles away from the fight. And he knew that now, if ever, was the time when his mother needed him. He knew how she felt: both of them knew that, whatever happened to Father in this fight, *they* had brought it about. They had acted for the best, as they saw it, but Tom knew that when soldiers and free traders met it would be a bloody affair, and Father was not the man to hang back.

He walked his horse quietly up the farm road and into the yard. All as still as the grave. As he had expected, everyone was off with the raiders, or well out of the way for safety. He dismounted and walked around the path to the back door. He had his hand on the latch when a quiet footstep behind him made him whip around, his heart giving a great swoop of fear.

A musket pointed straight at him. Holding it, his face white and set, his eyes staring, the slight, nondescript figure of Abel Marling.

"Aha! So here we are, Master Tom! Thought that was you skulking around the house. Here we are, creeping about spying again, eh? Going behind yer dad's back again."

Tom backed against the wall, his mind a blank with panic. The man had known him and been a friend all his life, but what did that signify? This minute Abel looked mad enough to shoot him like a rabbit. Keep still! Any quick jump, and that thing will go off. Keep him talking.

149

"I'm not spying, Abel. I'm going to see my mother. Don't you think she needs me today?"

"Maybe she does. But how did you *know* she did? Eh?"

Tom was silent, desperately searching for the right thing to say. If he told the truth, and his father came back victorious, what sort of life would she have? "I . . . I heard about it," he said at last.

"Ah. And if you heard about it, I lay you didn't keep it to yourself. I lay there's gaugers out there waiting for 'em. Well, this time the gaugers'll catch it. Master's got a whole blessed army, not just a few batmen."

It was time for some of the truth at least. "Abel, you don't understand. This time it's the finish. It's not a few gaugers waiting, it's a hundred dragoons. A hundred, Abel."

Abel's face went even whiter. "Gawd, you dirty sneaking little spy. You best say your prayers, Tom Gibbons, 'cause I'm going——"

"*Stay!*" The back door swung open, and Ethel Gibbons rushed out, her long graying brown hair down about her shoulders, her gown flying behind her. In a second she was planted in front of Tom, facing Marling, her arms out behind her to hold her son. "*I* was the spy, Abel. I made Tom go to them. *Made* him. He wouldn't at first. So shoot me, not Tom. Come, pull the trigger like a true free trading man and have done with it!"

For a full ten seconds the man stood leveling the musket at her. The end of the barrel, a little ring of metal, wavered slightly but still pointed straight at her breast. Then Marling half-turned, pitched the gun with a clatter on to the flint path, and sank down on to the low stone wall bordering the garden. He held his head in his hands; great sobs shook his whole body, and the tears ran through his fingers. At last the man had come out, had beaten down the free trader in him.

150

For a long time there was not a sound in the still cold dawn air but that of his terrible, wrenching sobs. Ethel Gibbons found no hate for him, only pity. She went to him, and raised him up gently. "Come, Abel. Come into the kitchen. I will pour you a cordial."

He let himself be led in, and sat down. He sipped the warm brandy-and-water, and shook his head. "I ain't good enough to come in here, mistress. Up on a gallows, I should be. Pointing a damned gun at you, what's been a true neighbor to me and my family all these years. And that lad there, what I taught to catch rabbits, and ride a horse and play a tune on a bit o' grass. Remember them bows and arrows I used to make, Master Tom, when you was a little old boy?"

"It is over, Abel, over. We have forgotten it already."

"Over! That's the word, mistress. Over. We've all been madmen round here. And murderers and all. No more killing, ma'am. No more dead men. Except one—*Toby Catt!*" The tears still ran in Marling's eyes, but his grief had turned into fury. "I don't know as I cared all that much for old man Hewett. But he was Polly's dad, and he could be a good old boy when he liked. Bit awkward as a rule, I know . . . She ain't ate a thing since he . . . went. If them soldiers catch Toby alive I'll see him hanged over the young dragoon, I will. I was there. I seen it all. I'll turn King's evidence on Toby Catt. We'll all be safer when he's kicking his heels in the air."

18. THE dragoon captain snapped his pocket-glass shut and ran down the stairs of the dwelling-house at Coldharbor Farm. Looking out across the flat, ruled level of the marsh, he had been able to follow the column ever since it emerged from the stacks and willows round Peasmarsh Farm. Now the last of the mounted figures had passed Coldharbor Farm gate. It was time to follow. Out in the yard, hidden from the road by a long barn, his men were already mounted, ready to move off in column of two's. Farmer Weaver and his family, still dazed and bewildered by their sudden imprisonment, watched from the front door; they saw the officer spring into his saddle at the head of the column, raise a white-gauntleted hand, and lead off down the track to the main road, his bugler bobbing at his side.

The free traders, making no attempt at any kind of concealment, wound along the marsh road at a brisk trot, laughing, shouting, talking in their excitement. "Now that's an odd thing, Toby," said Gibbons, as they passed Coldharbor Farm. "Jem Weaver said he would join us here today. Not like Jem to be out of a fight. Well, we've no time to wait for sluggards. He will have to catch up or miss the sport.

So will Abel Marling, too. He had only to saddle up his horse. But there, he's a slow fellow!"

On their right now was a chain of brackish, marshy pools called the Midrips; on their left Jury Gap Dyke, green-scummed, willow-lined, eight feet deep and eighteen wide. As they cleared the Midrips, another smaller dyke appeared in line with the road to their right.

They were in the trap; but they had not yet seen its terrible steel jaws.

Catt was riding, his head back, a flask of Schiedam gin at his mouth, when Gibbons pointed ahead with his crop. "Look, Toby, ahead there. What's all that dust?" The road ahead had no big bends, but snaked across the marsh in a sinewy way so that they could not see it far ahead. What they could see, in the first rays of sunlight, was a light could of gray dust riding above the pollarded willows. The dust was nearing them fast; in another half-minute it appeared round the bend ahead of them. Not a man of them but felt a wrench of fear as the golden, hazy sun picked out scarlet, white and glinting steel in the smoky cloud.

Robert Gibbons mastered his fear as soon as it rose in him. Betrayed again! But there was no turning back now! Besides, they were stronger in number than the soldiers, and what was more, dragoons didn't carry fire-arms. He half-turned, rose in his stirrups, and waved his musket high in the air. "To hell with the soldiers, lads! There's more of us. They shan't stop Sussex lads fighting for their rights!"

Even above the clatter of hoofs, they heard the clear notes of a bugle, and they saw the column of dragoons peeling off, wheeling left and right off the road to form a solid line between the two dykes. Promptly the smugglers broke into a canter, some going straight along the road, others plunging on to the marsh; they spurred at the soldiers, raising their muskets and firing as they rode. The volley was

153

ragged, but there were seventy of them, and their bullets hit the dragoons a shrewd blow. Down went half a dozen horses; suddenly a half a dozen other saddles were empty. Raw excisemen might have crumpled and fled, but these were seasoned troops; they had seen comrades fall before. What was more, they knew now that the worst was over: a musket is all very fine as a weapon if you have time to aim and reload. But the smugglers had wasted nearly all their advantage, for a man on a cantering horse cannot possibly aim his first shot well. And the dragoons were determined that they should not have a second. Having no guns, they had been sitting ducks so far. But they had steel, and the smugglers should soon feel it! The bugle sounded again, forty bright sabers flashed in the sun, and the line of troopers, its gaps now closed, moved forward steadily in perfect line. Gibbons saw that fearful line moving inexorably forward, and knew, with a sinking heart, that he and his men could not break it, for many had only useless muskets now, and there were few good swordsmen among the rest. If only the fools had kept still and aimed properly! Everything was going to pieces. This was where a bugle and some discipline would have been priceless. He wheeled his horse and bellowed as loudly as he could: "Back to cover, boys, and reload. We'll pepper their scarlet coats for them yet!"

He turned his horse back towards Peasmarsh, and his hope, his courage, his will drained away in a second, leaving him for the moment a weak shell. Now at last he saw the trap. Right across the strip of marsh between the dykes was a line of dragoons, the exact mirror-like counterpart of the first! Where the devil had they come from? It was as if they had sprung up out of the rich black marsh soil! Five minutes ago the free traders had been an invincible column of armed men riding on a nearly defenseless Customs House; now they were seventy disorganized and bewildered men, milling about on a narrow rectangle of marsh, with no cover, no room, no way out, no time to reload muskets; above all, no time for him to think. Both lines of dragoons, their sabers raised, were moving forward at a steady walk; every moment the space between them was shrinking.

Never mind! No surrender! He had some of the toughest lads in the south with him; they still had their pistols and swords. He swung his horse back again towards Hythe; better to charge the troops who had already been mauled by their musket-fire. He waved his sword aloft. "Barkers and swords, lads! This way! At 'em again!" They wheeled, and in a great ragged wedge, its point moving along the road, they charged towards the east; as they did so a bugle sounded behind them, and the troopers from Coldharbor broke into a trot. The free traders hit the line at full gallop and the troopers staggered back yards in the middle at the crushing impact. But this was what the dragoons had been trained for; the line held, and the troopers on the wings closed in on each side of the struggling mass of men. The soldiers' faces, grim and wooden under their polished helmets, gave no sign of any feeling, but in fact the men were enraged at the butchery of their mates, and they began to hack away with their terrible heavy chopping swords, against which the lighter blades of the smugglers were of little use. More troopers went down as horse-pistols banged at point-blank range, but at the same moment the other line of dragoons took the smugglers in the rear; and half of them were forced to face about and fight for their lives to keep away those great downward axe-like blows of the sabers. Soon the smugglers found themselves herded into a circle, facing outwards at the ring of big, red-coated men on huge chargers—men whose red swords rose and fell, men who kept, foot by foot, moving forward all the time, penning them tighter and tighter.

Iorwerth Lewis sat on his horse beside Colonel Westbroke,

a little way off from the fighting on the Lydd road. He had never seen a hand-to-hand battle before, and was shocked at the senseless butchery going on. Suddenly, amid the yells and screams he heard his name screeched in a high crazy voice, and there was Catt, breaking out of the ring and galloping towards him, pistol leveled. Catt fired and Lewis felt a blow and a stab of pain in his left side. He had time to think: "He's hit me. I shall fall." But he did not fall; instead, he found himself looking down his own loaded pistol at Catt. The range was a foot or two; he could not miss. God knew he hated and loathed the man enough to kill him, but he did not. He kept control of his forefinger. Let the creature stand trial and hang as an example to all. To kill him might make him a local hero. "No!" he shouted to a pursuing trooper, whose raised saber was about to come down on Catt's back. "No, soldier! Take him prisoner and lead him away. Bind him and take him back to where my men are waiting with the wagon."

The battle had now broken up and spread, like knots of men hacking and stabbing at each other over the whole slice of marsh. Now and then a dismounted smuggler, making a desperate run for the dyke and safety, was hunted and cut down from behind by a dragoon, the trooper leaning from the saddle to chop with contemptuous ease. The soldiers were now possessed with the murdering madness of battle; the mind of each of them narrowed to one red thought—kill! Lewis caught sight of Gibbons, a tall figure, his bright blue coat slashed to ribbons, fighting hand-to-hand with a dragoon sergeant.

Even Colonel Westbroke, who had seen such scenes and worse scores of times, was appalled at this slaughter of Englishmen by Englishmen. It was time to stop. He barked at his bugler: "Sound the Retreat!" The man looked surprised, but the silvery, cutting notes rang out, and the dragoons, breaking off their combats, retired to form up again in the lines, facing inwards to a small square of marsh now littered with the bodies of free traders. Since the first volley only one or two soldiers had been killed, though most had been marked somewhere. The smugglers, on the other hand, had been cut to pieces: a good thirty lay still, never to move again; riderless horses ran terrified here and there; the surviving raiders were dazed, exhausted, shattered by the cruel slaughter, nearly all wounded about the head and shoulders by those fearful blades.

The Colonel raised his voice: "Gibbons! If you are the leader of this party, order your men to put down all weapons and give themselves up for arrest and trial. I warn you, Gibbons, that if you refuse, not one of you will leave this field alive."

Robert Gibbons looked all around him. Barely half past six on a perfect summer's day—a Sunday too—and yet since dawn his whole world and life had crashed in ruin. He heard a distant sound of bleating; he looked beyond the Jury Gap Dyke and saw the white sheep thickly flecking the wide green sea of Romney Marsh, the flat rich sea on which he and his fathers had lived out their lives. He saw the miles of grass and water and waving willows as if for the first time; and yet he knew it was the last time too. He looked down; there on the red turf, almost under his horse's feet, a dead man lay flat and stared up at the drifting fluffy clouds. Young Peter Noakes. Only nineteen.

It was time to give up.

It was a month later. The last day's session of Rye Assizes was finishing, and the packed courtroom was emptying into the streets, where heavy summer rain fell. The water streamed thickly down the window of the lawyer's room in the courthouse. Nicholas Mole led the way in, and showed Ethel Gibbons, pale but dry-eyed, to a chair, fussing over her while Tom and Mary found themselves seats. The door opened again, and Lord Tillingham came in, followed by Lewis. The Welshman had recovered from his wound, but looked very unlike a man who had just won a battle; he had seen too much of the cost of victory, both on the field and now in the home. Here was a woman who might well never see her husband again, children who were now fatherless.

His lordship made a bow. "Madam, we should not dream of intruding on your grief for more than a moment. Mr. Lewis and I are here merely to thank you from our hearts for the truly noble part you have played in this terrible affair. For myself, if there is anything in my power which would be of service to you, you know you have only to ask. But to tell the truth, I do not feel you are alone in the world when you have the company of your daughter, and the support of such a man as Tom. I must lose a budding librarian, I see, but you will gain a son who has proved himself to all the world."

Mrs. Gibbons smiled her thanks, and held out her hand to both men; as Lewis took it, she said, "I have heard so much about you from Tom, Mr. Lewis. I hope we shall see much of you at Peasmarsh?"

"It is good of you, ma'am, but I fear I am leaving this part of the kingdom. We Welshmen, you must understand, become very restless in exile. We begin to feel a longing for our native soil. *Hiraeth* is our word for it. Now that this is over, I shall try to obtain another teaching post, this time in Wales. However, I shall not be leaving for a week or so, and I shall be delighted to visit you." He looked at Mary in a way that made her flush and drop her eyes. "Yes, delighted, ma'am."

When the two men were gone, Mole cleared his throat importantly. "Now, Mrs. Gibbons, as to your question: as your husband's attorney, I cannot countenance an appeal. Ten years in the plantations in Van Diemen's Land is bad enough, no doubt, but it could have been worse. I will be plain with you, ma'am: for such an armed insurrection as this, judges have been known to hang every man taken. As it is, only Catt is to hang, and that for the murder of the dragoon in March; appeal judges have the power to *increase* as well as decrease a sentence. I must advise you most earnestly, ma'am, against risking another trial. Your husband was, after all, the leader of the insurrection. Besides, he is a strong man in his prime; you may yet live happily together again. The Van Diemen's Land plantations will be a bitter pill to a free man, a man in your husband's position in society, but I have heard that some of the released convicts have done wonderfully well, settling a new colony. Ten years will pass, Mrs. Gibbons . . ."

His smooth, smug voice droned on. Much he cares, Tom was thinking; he will soon find another freighter to supply him his brandy and tea and lace and silk. Tom's mind went back to the brief, heart-wrenching scene in the little gray cell in the courthouse basement after the sentence had been passed. His father, his face still marked by long saber-scars, holding him by the shoulders. "You were right all along, Tom. I've had time to think, this last month. God forgive me, I hated you enough at one time. But you were right and I was wrong. Times change, and a man must change with them. D'you remember the day we were going to market, and you said, 'Can't we just be farmers?' Now it's you who'll have to be the farmer." He frowned as a thought struck him. "By the by, look to the sheep well now; this thundery weather brings out the blow-fly like the devil. Don't forget those two rafters in the barn that need replacing. Oh, and the old hay in there—don't let them use it for the horses; it's too musty—you'll have them all broken-winded. And the shepherd told me——" He checked himself with a smile; his eyes watered. "But why do I rattle on so? You'll do well enough. And look after your mother, Tom. She'll need you now to make up for the fool she married."